STAR STRIKER #3

# THE
# FINAL
# GOAL

STAR STRIKER #3

# THE
# FINAL
# GOAL

## MARY AMATO

HOLIDAY HOUSE • NEW YORK

Copyright © 2023 by Mary Amato

All Rights Reserved

HOLIDAY HOUSE is registered in the U.S. Patent and Trademark Office.

Printed and bound in September 2023 at Maple Press, York, PA, USA.

www.holidayhouse.com

First Edition

1 3 5 7 9 10 8 6 4 2

Library of Congress Cataloging-in-Publication Data

Names: Amato, Mary, author.

Title: The final goal / Mary Amato.

Description: First edition. | New York : Holiday House, 2023. | Series:
Star striker ; #3 | Audience: Ages 8-12. | Audience: Grades 4-6. |
Summary: Albert, Star Striker for the Zeenods, and his alien teammates
face the final game of the interplanetary soccer tournament and confront
the empire that wants to defeat them once and for all.

Identifiers: LCCN 2023006593 | ISBN 9780823449132 (hardcover)

Subjects: CYAC: Human-alien encounters—Fiction. | Soccer—Fiction. |
Sports tournaments—Fiction. | Science fiction. | LCGFT: Sports fiction.
| Science fiction. | Novels.

Classification: LCC PZ7.A49165 Fi 2023 | DDC [Fic]—dc23

LC record available at https://lccn.loc.gov/2023006593

ISBN: 978-0-8234-4913-2 (hardcover)

With gratitude, for Simon Amato and
the Life of Gains

The old way is to lead with invulnerability and enlist followers. The new way is to lead with full humanity — and cultivate a team of leaders.
— Abby Wambach

# 1.0

On Monday, January 20, at precisely 10:03 a.m., Star Striker Albert Kinney was crouched at the edge of a dock staring with terror into the silvery-black water of the Patuxent River in the state of Maryland on planet Earth.

He was on a half-day environmental education field trip with his fellow seventh graders and was supposed to be counting the number of tiny fish in the bucket of ice-cold water he had hauled up, to see if the river's pollution was decreasing. Instead, he was lost in thought, thinking about his upcoming johka practice on the planet Gaböq that afternoon and worrying about how much danger was lurking ahead.

He had read about Gaböq. Fissures in Gaböq's johka fields could crack open if the temperature grew too hot, which meant that johka players could fall through the cracks and plunge into the cold waterways called under-rivers that ran in a network of caverns beneath the fields. Because Albert was a terrible swimmer, knowing he could fall into an underground river during a johka game was frightening enough. But Gaböq's under-rivers were full of creatures called grythers, which were like electric eels. Giant, deadly electric eels.

And there was more. His rivals—entire planets full of aliens—wanted him gone for good. Since Albert had accepted the challenge to become the Star Striker for planet Zeeno, he had been bombed, hurtled into a black hole, kidnapped, given poison, shot at, and almost slurped into the mouth of a flying predator. An assassin had even been sent to Earth. And he knew there were more attacks to come. The Tevs and their allies were determined to get rid of him and so was the Zeenod botmaker Mehk. Albert had no idea where Mehk was, but if Albert didn't quit the tournament, Mehk would hunt him down and make sure he quit.

And on top of all that, there was an additional, ridiculous worry. On the way to the field trip, his classmate Gabby had announced that she was having a secret Valentine's Day party at her house next month. At night. Her parents wouldn't be home, she had said with a huge grin. She had invited about ten friends—including Albert—and said that each of them could come with someone. Like a date, she had said with another grin. And then Freddy had elbowed him and whispered, "I'll ask Min if you ask Jessica."

That kind of social pressure was the last thing Albert needed at a time like this. He closed his eyes and thought about the Z-da that he wore around his neck and tucked under his shirt. He wished he could pull out the pendant right now, activate a szoŭ, and hibernate in a hygg until March. Or April. Or next year.

Along the dock were Albert's classmates huddled in their winter coats, recording observations about their buckets of river water on clipboards, blowing on their fingers to keep them warm, and chattering about the party.

Jessica noticed Albert's stillness. Assuming he was spacing out, and thinking it would be funny to startle him, she gestured to Gabby and Min to follow her. Silently the three crept up behind Albert.

When they were close enough to touch him, they stood still, grinning at each other in disbelief because he still hadn't noticed them. In slow motion, Jessica reached out to tap Albert on the shoulder, and Gabby whispered, "Boo."

Albert freaked. He lunged forward, arms flailing, and fell.

Many people in life-threatening predicaments have observed that time seems to slow down in a moment of crisis, and this was true for Albert. As he fell toward the surface of the water, the thought occurred to him that if he died, at least he wouldn't have to go to Gabőq. At the same time, he could hear Jessica's voice behind him calling his name, and he knew he had overreacted to nothing more than a prank.

Too late.

Down he plunged into the icy depths.

On the dock, it looked to the girls as if Albert had sunk like a stone. Gabby screamed, and Min sprinted to get a teacher while Jessica stood staring at the surface of the water in shock, waiting for Albert to come up for air.

Come on, Albert, she chanted silently, come on!

As students gathered, Jessica grabbed an oar from a rowboat on the other side of the dock and slipped it into the water right where Albert had fallen in.

3

"He disappeared?" Trey's voice behind Jessica sounded shaky.

"The water's freezing!" Gabby screamed. "He's going to die. Oh my God, he's going to die!"

As Trey ran to get another oar, Jessica got down on her stomach so she could sink the oar deeper in. Back and forth she moved it.

Come on, Albert, she kept chanting, hoping she'd feel his sudden grip.

Seconds passed. And then more seconds. All she felt against the oar was the dense weight of the river itself.

# 1.1

At the same moment that Albert toppled into the water, another drama was playing out nearby. None other than the infamous botmaker Mehklen Pahck was hiding out in an alley behind a cluster of restaurants in Albert's hometown.

The frustrated Zeenod was wearing clothes he had stolen to disguise himself as an Earthling—pants that were too small and boots that were too big topped off with a grimy parka and ski mask. Sitting on the filthy pavement, he was talking to a large garbage can on wheels as if it were a listening companion. Actually, he wasn't talking to the can. He was talking to the mangled masterpiece that was his robot, which was stuffed inside the can.

"I wish I could take off these clothes," he said, reaching inside the ski mask to scratch his cheek. "Three hundred thousand years of evolution and these idiot Earthlings haven't been able to invent decent smartfabric." He stopped and stared at the can. "Should we return to the ITV? I thought I could sneak into a robotics facility here on Earth to fix you. But I haven't been able to find a decent one."

Silence.

He began hitting himself on the side of the head. "Think. Think. Think. Lat and the Tevs and Z-Tevs are definitely looking for us. It is quite possible that, by now, they have tracked my ITV and will be waiting to kill me if we return. But!" His stomach growled. He closed his eyes, feeling the pang of hunger compete with his piercing headache. "Earth was a mistake. Let's take the risk and return to Zeeno." He stood up, unzipped his parka, and pulled out his Z-da.

And, at that very moment, a feeling came over him that he was not alone. He turned to see two guys approaching. Earthlings, of course. Males. Late teens, Mehk guessed.

"He's talking to the trash," one guy said, and they both started laughing.

Alarmed, Mehk tried to slip his Z-da pendant back into hiding, but the teens caught a glimpse of the gold and leaped into action. One pinned Mehk's arms back while the other yanked the pendant from his neck. Before he could blink, they were gone.

Leaving his masterpiece behind, Mehk chased after them, but by the time he rounded the corner, they were speeding off on a motorbike.

He stood, stunned. His only way off the planet, gone.

# 1.2

Full-on panic!

Dragged down by his heavy boots, jeans, and jacket, Albert sank deeper into the water. He tried to move his arms and kick his legs, but his muscles seized, and he was sure the freezing temperature would send his heart into cardiac arrest. His hand brushed against something slimy, and he recoiled, opening his eyes in the murky water. As soon as he did, he realized that something about him was different. Although the water was dark and cloudy, it didn't bother his eyes at all. He blinked. The Z-da he wore on a cord tucked under his shirt had come out. Quickly he grabbed the pendant and shoved it back to keep it safe. And then he stopped moving. Wait. The temperature. It felt cold, but not deadly cold.

To help him adapt on other planets, the Zeenods had given him all kinds of protective treatments—skin spray and eye drops. Those treatments were regulating his body temperature and helping him here, he realized. And the breathing implant in his nose and throat! He remembered reading in his guide that it would enable him to breathe underwater.

Albert, he said to himself, you're safe. Stop panicking.

He tried to calm down, imagining how amazing it would be to take off swimming. All his life, he had been afraid of the water—one of his worst shawbles—but now he wouldn't have to worry about his lungs or the cold. Just relax and try to breathe, he told himself. But every human instinct in his very human body refused to let him open his mouth.

In the next second, something dark and firm and strange swam through the murky water toward him. He panicked again, flailing to get away from it, but the thing followed him and brushed against him, and suddenly he realized it was an oar. He grabbed on and was immediately pulled upward.

As he broke through the surface of the water, he gasped for air. Staring at him on the dock were Jessica and Trey, surrounded by the rest of the seventh graders, his biology teacher, and several adult chaperones, including Jessica's dad, who was also Albert's clarinet teacher, Mr. Sam.

Believing that he was in danger of hypothermia, the teacher quickly rushed Albert into Mr. Sam's car. A chaperone hurried over with Albert's phone, which had been confiscated on the bus. Before Albert could protest, he was being driven to the hospital.

"Holy moly," Mr. Sam blurted out. "I am not good in emergencies, Albert. I never should have volunteered. You must be so cold—Wait! Heat! Sorry!" He blasted the heater and glanced nervously at Albert while he screeched onto the main road. "Take off your wet jacket. Here, put mine on…" He started taking off his jacket with one hand while the other gripped the wheel. "Holy moly. This is terrible. Do you know where you are? Can you talk? Hypothermia can shut down your brain and—"

"I think I'm okay," Albert said, taking the jacket. "Really. Thanks."

Mr. Sam glanced again at Albert. "But you were under for so long!"

The mention of time reminded Albert that he had a practice to attend. He touched his chest to make sure he could feel the Z-da. Still there. Good. The Zeenods were counting on him. He had been planning to initiate the szoŭ once they had returned to school. But there was no way he could do that while being examined in a hospital emergency room.

"I don't need a hospital," Albert said. "I really am fine. See? I'm not shivering or turning blue or anything."

Mr. Sam looked at the wet hand Albert had extended toward him.

Uncertain, Mr. Sam asked him to call home. Knowing his mom would freak out, Albert called his grandma. Luckily, she picked up. Always calm in emergencies, Nana gave the okay for Mr. Sam to bring him home.

When they pulled up, Albert's faithful partner and next-door neighbor trotted to the gate. Seeing Tackle jump up as they parked filled Albert with warmth. What a dog. Always on the lookout. A feeling of gratitude swept over Albert. Yes, his mission as Star Striker had put him in danger, but it had also given him new abilities, the most joyful of which was to be able to understand the language of Dog.

*You smell like dead fish. What are you doing home?* Tackle barked before Albert even had the car door closed. *Another assassination attempt?*

Nana hustled out to see if he was okay and to thank Mr. Sam, which meant that all Albert could do at the moment was whisper the word *later* to Tackle under his breath.

"Okay, kiddo," Nana said, putting an arm around him as they walked inside. "Let's do a brain-function check. What's your name?"

"Albert."

"What's your sister's name?"

"Erin."

"What's three hundred plus three hundred?"

"Four thousand."

She gave him a look.

"Just kidding, Nana."

She smiled and put a hand on his forehead. "You feel a little slimy but fine. Take a long hot shower and then a nap. You're probably wiped out. I'll want to hear everything, but that can wait."

Albert breathed a sigh of relief. The nap would be his cover. Nana never bothered him when his door was closed. Thanks to time-folding, all he needed was twenty-seven minutes to get to practice and back. He didn't want to go, but he couldn't let his teammates down.

As he reached his room, a text interrupted his thoughts.

*Really really really didn't mean for you to fall in!!!!!!!!!!!!!!!!!!*
*Seriously sorry. I owe you. What would make up for it? Chocolate?*

Albert smiled. That had to be Jessica. They hadn't exchanged numbers yet, but it had to be her.

Maybe he should just ask her to the party right then and there, he thought, but then he told himself she was just being nice. Just because someone is nice and friendly and funny and interesting and has an amazing smile doesn't mean that person wants to go to a Valentine's Day party with you. What if he asked her and she just said yes because she felt like she owed him? He wrote back.

*Hey, thanks. I'm really really really okay.*

A second later, another text arrived.

*Thanks! Can you hang out after your lesson on Thursday?*

Albert couldn't believe it. Another text from Jessica. This was better than okay. He thought through all the possible responses. Yes. Yeah. Sure. I think so. Definitely. See ya. Then he wrote:

*Since there are no rivers, lakes, oceans, or swimming pools near your house, I guess it's safe to say yes.*

He stared at the screen, heart thumping. And then her reply came:

*haha. Very funny. I mean actually. You made me laugh. Mr. Ellis is about to take my phone. Bye!*

He and Jessica Atwater were texting. This was momentous. Definitely worth the fall.

# 1.3

Tackle stood at the gate, sniffing the air. *Grrrr.* Why had Albert returned wet and fishy-smelling? Did one of Zeeno's enemies send an assassin down to drown Albert? *Grrrr.* Albert shouldn't be going on field trips. Shouldn't be going to school. Shouldn't be leaving home. At all. Too dangerous.

*Sniff.* There was the odor Albert had left behind. And there was another smell. Bananas and man-sweat. That was left behind by the workman who had fixed the Pattersons' gate that morning. Nothing else in the air that seemed out of the ordinary.

The dog pushed against the new locking mechanism with his nose. *Grrrr.* A new lock! Just what he didn't need. If the Pattersons would just leave the gate unlocked, he could go in and out as he pleased for his patrols and keep them all safe. They should trust that he wouldn't run away.

To shake off his frustration, he took a lap in the yard around the house and then another at an even speedier clip. Felt good to get the muscles working. Important to stay in shape. To stay loose and fast. He leaped over a flowerpot and jumped up on the picnic table and back down. A little obstacle course. Loose and fast.

Suddenly he stopped. His snout lifted. A new smell! Or was it an old smell? A dangerous smell? He couldn't tell. His ears twitched and his hackles rose, and then he took off toward the front and jumped up, putting his paws on the gate and taking in another big sniff.

The street was empty. He sniffed again. The wind shifted and the smell grew more intense. Complex. Old food. Damp clothes? Metal. Pine.

And then something or someone moved behind an SUV parked on the street two houses down from Albert's house. He knew the SUV. It was always parked there. That wasn't the problem. But there was definitely movement behind it. Someone or something was crouching behind it.

He barked twice and then growled, not taking his eyes off the spot.

Then there was a flurry of movement. A man, or what looked like a man, raced away, pulling a large garbage can behind him.

Tackle went crazy, barking and pawing the gate. Who was that? *Grrrr.* Definitely suspicious! He raced over to the side yard and barked at Albert's bedroom window. *Albert, get out here!*

The bedroom window opened. *Shhh! I'm going to practice,* Albert whispered. *I just activated the szoŭ. What's going on?*

*Someone was just in front of your house. I don't like it. Come over here and open my gate, Albert!*

11

*I can't,* Albert whispered. *I'm about to get beamed up. Keep watch—*

In the next second, Tackle heard a familiar crackling sound and saw the eerie shimmer of UV light in the sky above the house, and then Albert was gone.

# 1.4

With a handheld device in one of its tentacles, Unit K7721359 scanned Albert as he materialized. "One hundred percent Albert Kinney."

Since Albert's previous ITV had crashed under suspicious circumstances right before the last game, the Fŭigor Jokha Federation had supplied him with a new ITV and a new robotic chaperone. This new robot had been designed by the Zhidorians and looked like one. It had two heads, tentacles instead of arms, and smartskin with a wet, plump look. The eyes of one of its two heads focused on Albert. The other head was focused on the ITV's main control panel. "Takeoff for Gabŏq will begin in precisely forty-seven seconds."

Unit K clearly had not been programmed for human small talk, the comfort of which Albert needed at the moment.

"I have a request," Albert said. "Let's say hello when we see each other. My name is Albert, you know."

"Hello, Albert You Know," Unit K repeated.

"No. Just Albert!" Albert groaned.

"Just Albert it is," the robot said.

Albert sat down and buckled his seat belt. If his coach, Kayko, and his teammate Giac had designed this robot, it would have been way smarter. And if Mehk had designed it, the thing would be one hundred percent lifelike. Thinking about the talented Zeenods and how much the Tevs and Z-Tevs had taken from them brought Albert's mind back to his duties as Star Striker. And so, for the rest of the journey, Albert focused on preparing for practice. He spent time either reading about Gaböq in his guide or else hydrating and hibernating in the hygg. Although the trip was fast and quiet, it wasn't exactly relaxing. What he learned about Gaböq reminded him just how challenging the geography would be, and by the time he arrived, the knots in his stomach had grown and tightened.

Unit K, who stood silently near the doorway as Albert prepared to exit, wasn't any help. One head was gazing at the rear of the spacecraft and the other was staring straight out the door.

"It would be nice if at least one of your heads would say encouraging things to me," Albert said. "At least at the start or end of a trip."

The robot paused, eyes in both heads blinking rapidly.

Albert was just thinking that the large, deep brown, wide-set eyes reminded him of cow eyes when one head swiveled toward Albert. "Can you utter an example, Albert?"

Albert shrugged. "Say something like *You got this, Albert.*"

Unit K's head tilted. "That sentence is grammatically incorrect. The correct way to say this would be: *You have the skills necessary to achieve success, Albert.*"

Albert sighed. "Does it have to be so formal? Can you access language in your files that's more relaxed? You know, slang, like *Hey, what's up?* My nana calls it shooting the breeze."

The eyes-blinking thing happened again. "Program is modifying to integrate American slang related to *shooting the breeze*," both heads said at the same time. And then the head closest to Albert turned and said, "Golly gee, Albert! You sure are a swell pal." The other head swiveled and said, "Those Zeenods are lucky ducks to have a guy like you on their side!"

Albert laughed. "I think that's slang from when my grandma was a kid."

"You're the cat's meow, Albert!" the robot said. "You're the coolest cat in town!"

"Oh man, do I wish I could be videorecording this," Albert said. "This would absolutely go viral."

One of Unit K's robotic tentacles reached out and opened the door. "It's time you make like a banana and split!" The other head added, "Time to skedaddle!"

Albert laughed again, but as he descended the hatch stairs the lightness of his mood was quickly replaced with dread. Unlike the arrival ceremonies on both Zeeno and Jhaateez, there was only his team waiting for him at the doorway of the practice facility. No welcome from the Gaböqs. No words from their president. No projection of his johkadin card or the johkadin card of Xutu. No throngs of fans asking for holo-autographs.

The practice facility was a gray granite structure with intricate carvings on its surface, and it was surrounded by other buildings, all similar in appearance. Surrounding the cityscape was the landscape of Gaböq—flat land, dry and reddish in color, with huge gray boulders here and there that looked as if they had been dropped from above. Above it all, the sky was full of active, angry-looking clouds, and yet the air was hot and dry.

No Gaböqs were in sight, but their distinctive footprints were everywhere. Huge impressions baked into the reddish crust of the ground. Two feet in the front and one in the back.

As he walked from the ITV to join his teammates, he noticed that phrases were stamped into the ground within the footprints. He bent down for a quick examination, and the moment he realized what the Gaböq letters spelled out, he wished his language-translation implant weren't so effective. Different sets of footprints had different messages, but they all had the same structure and vibe.

**ZEENODS=LOSERS**
**AK=DUST**
**ZEENODS=CORPSES**
**AK=DEATH**

A chill went up Albert's spine. AK had to stand for Albert Kinney.

"Albert! Welcome!" his teammates called out. After hugs and fist bumps, Ennjy explained that they needed to discuss how to find Mehk, and get that spybot with evidence about Lat's crimes to the Fŭigor Interplanetary Council, but first they had to make use of their time in the practice facility.

"Wait," Albert said. "What's all this?" He gestured to the strange in-ground graffiti.

"Ah," Feeb said. "A Gaböq custom. They cut messages into their feet because they believe that stamping those messages into the ground will make the words come true."

"What!"

"Gaböq skin is unusually thick and regrows rapidly," Toben explained. "They cut new messages into their feet frequently."

"They hope we're going to die?" Albert gasped. "That's so harsh!"

"Don't think about it," Doz said. "Let's roll and rock."

Shaken, Albert tried to keep his head up as he followed his team inside.

After the ahn ritual, they warmed up on the indoor practice field, and both activities helped to ease Albert's anxiety. There were no icy rims to skate on and no zee eruptions to ride, and so the way johka was played here was much more like soccer on Earth. For the first few minutes of running and passing drills, Albert felt his confidence increase. It was hot, yes, the kind of hot that could quickly sap energy, and the lack of grass took a little getting used to, but other than that, the play all felt good and normal.

That didn't last long, though. Soon enough, Ennjy made an announcement that Albert didn't like.

"Time for drills with the fissures," she said.

Giac turned to Albert. "In the stadium, the fissures will occur naturally. We won't know when or where. But in here we can control them the way we can control the zees in the practice facility on Zeeno."

"Let's show Albert," Ennjy said. Using a remote controller, she pointed at a spot on the field, and a crack appeared and widened until it was about three feet wide and six feet long. "They're usually one to five feet wide and six to seven feet long."

"It's an actual gap in the ground," Albert said, shocked to see it, although he had been warned.

Doz and a few other players ran over to it. "Ah, feel the cool!" Doz said, leaning over to feel the cool air that was coming up from the cavern below.

"The ground won't collapse?" Albert ventured a little closer to peer into the dark opening. The musty smell rising from the fissure sent another chill up his spine.

"The structure of the ground here is highly complex," Giac said. "Nothing like the ground on Earth. This can handle a huge amount of weight, even up to the edge of a fissure."

Albert glanced up at Giac, sure that if she had the time she would want to give him a full scientific explanation. "I think I read that the under-river is about thirty feet below?"

Giac nodded.

"You're right," Feeb said. "And the river itself is about eighteen feet deep."

Doz leaned down and yelled, "Helloooooo!" and his echo resounded.

"The Gaböqs love fissures. They plunge all the way down and use their main leg to bounce all the way back up."

Albert had seen footage. It was unbelievably quick. A Gaböq would disappear and then come flying back up. That leg must be built like a powerful pogo stick, Albert thought.

"We deal with fissures in several different ways," Ennjy explained. "First of all, if one occurs ahead of you and it isn't too wide, you can easily jump across it." She used the remote to make the opening too narrow to fall through. "Just make sure you don't trip."

"But if it's too wide to jump across?" Albert asked.

Sormie chimed in. "If a fissure is wide but it's ahead of me, I usually pass the ball over it to a teammate on the other side of it. Then I run around it." Her smile was shy. "I don't like taking the risk of falling."

"Let's show him," Ennjy said, and widened the same fissure so that it was about five by seven. Sormie demonstrated, passing the ball over the crack to Reeda, who was still on the other side. Reeda passed it back to Giac, who was next to Albert.

"But if you don't kick it hard enough, the ball could fall in, right?" Albert said.

"Not a johka ball." Giac kicked the ball lightly toward the gap. Just when gravity should have taken it downward, the ball stopped in midair, hovering over the gap. "The smart technology of a johka ball means that it will never fall in. It can get stuck, though, over an opening, as you can see."

"How do you get it?" Albert said.

"However you can," Feeb said. "And hopefully before a Gabőq beats you to it."

Toben backed up to get a running start, and then he leaped, managing to kick the ball as he jumped across the fissure.

The list of everything Albert needed to practice was whirling through his brain. He knew he could jump that far on solid ground but wondered if seeing the gap would make his body freeze. He'd have to work through the fear factor.

"Of course, a fissure can cause problems even if you don't have the ball. One can open up as you're defending or running," Ennjy said. "We have tricks to keep from falling in. Show him, Doz."

Doz grinned and then shocked Albert by jumping into the gaping hole. His bem flew up and out, extending and snagging on the top of the crusty crack with a firm grip. Amazed, Albert peered over to see his friend dangling, his capelike bem keeping him from plunging down.

"Unbelievable. What now?" Albert asked.

Using his fierce core, Doz swung like a gymnast, tucking his legs up and flipping back onto safe ground.

"If our minds are right and we can respond quickly enough, we can keep from falling all the way down," Ennjy said as Doz's bem retracted.

"You?" Doz patted Albert's bemless back. "You'll probably just go down."

"Sorry!" Sormie added with a wince.

Albert wondered how his predecessor, the former Star Striker Lightning Lee, had handled these fissures, but he didn't ask, afraid that hearing about Lee's skills would just make him feel worse.

"Albert, your concern about the fissures is not a shawble. It is understandable," the ever-intuitive Ennjy said. "The fissures are dangerous. This is why we are here—to practice."

Feeb stepped forward. "Albert, just remember, the grythers down there—"

"There are eels down there?" Albert interrupted, peering again into the gaping hole.

"Animatronic grythers for the sake of practice," Feeb said. "Not real ones. These won't sting you, but if you provoke them, they are programmed to touch you and those touches will be recorded so you can keep track of how well you are responding to the experience."

"They're not as beautiful as the real ones," Toben added.

Albert stared at the keeper. "You think the real ones are beautiful?"

Sormie grimaced. "I don't like them. But Toben thinks all animals are beautiful."

"You don't have to fear them," Toben said. "Remember, they're blind. If you remain calm and swim gently to the surface and then float with the current until you see the exit hatch, they won't bother you."

"If you kick or splash around a lot, they will attack, though!" Sormie said. "They dislike agitation. If they sense those types of vibrations in the water, they'll assume you are attacking and they'll sting you."

"You might want to activate the glow-light function of your uniform, Albert," Heek said. "If I go down, I like having a little light."

"Good point, Heek," Ennjy said, and showed Albert how to turn the glow function on and off. "The smartfabric will adjust automatically to darkness. Let's send someone down with Al—"

Before Ennjy could finish her sentence, Doz jumped forward. "Me!"

Ennjy smiled. "On the count of five?"

It was all happening too fast. Albert's heart was pounding so loudly, he could hardly hear the countdown. Just when he was going to protest, there was a gentle push, and he was falling.

*Aaaaahhhh!* Down he plunged into the cold water. Panicking, Albert forgot everything he had just learned and immediately kicked his way to the surface.

As he broke through, he noticed that the smartfabric of his uniform was giving off light. The glow bounced off the walls and cast an eerie glow. On the right Albert could see Doz's body floating face down, as still as a corpse.

"Doz!" Albert cried out, splashing toward him.

Doz's head turned slightly. "Be chilled, Albert! Float your boat. Remember, your implant will allow you to breathe underwater. It feels refreshing, doesn't it?" Doz turned his face back into the water.

Although Albert knew he should float, his arms and legs kept thrashing. If he could just get over to what looked like a rocky ledge on one side of the under-river, he could climb up and out of the water. But in the next second he saw a dark shape, the size of a firefighter's hose, slithering toward him on the water's surface. A gryther! He changed direction and saw another coming for him. Treading water, he thrashed around to head the other way, and there were six more. He screamed, and then the eels were on him.

*Zap! Zap! Zap!* Simulations of the sounds of stings came from speakers in the tops of the eels' heads. *Zap! Zap! Zap!*

Ennjy's voice called down. "Stop moving, Albert, and they'll stop attacking!"

Unable to stay calm, Albert kept trying to escape as the slithering snake heads kept bumping against his arms, legs, and face. He knew they weren't real, weren't stinging him, but he couldn't shake the fear, and his legs and arms were losing strength. No longer able to hold himself up, Albert went under, every instinct in his body keeping his mouth shut. He opened his eyes to see the tangle of eel bodies in every direction. And then he saw Doz swimming toward him. The grythers paused to take in the new activity, but Doz swam calmly through the tangle and pulled Albert up.

As they broke through the surface, a robotic voice made a loud, humiliating announcement that echoed through the entire cavern: "Simulation complete. Player is dead. Reset program to try again."

The eels went rigid and sank out of sight. Too exhausted to swim, Albert let Doz pull him to the exit.

# 1.5

"Hey, buddy. I bet you had a nifty time with your pals," Unit K said, one tentacle waving a greeting as Albert boarded the ITV.

Numb with humiliation, Albert commanded the robot to return to his usual way of talking, and then he crawled into his hygg. All he wanted to do was get back to Earth.

Knowing that the Pattersons were gone, Albert asked Unit K to set the return szoǔ coordinates for Tackle's backyard. As soon as he beamed down and saw his faithful friend running out his dog door to greet him, tears welled in his eyes. He blinked them back and tried to control his emotions.

*I smelled you coming!* Tackle said, jumping on Albert to give him some love. *Glad to have you back safe and sound. I've been on edge. How was practice?*

*Terrible,* Albert said. He sat on the steps of the back porch, and when Tackle nuzzled in for a hug, something in Albert broke loose.

*Let it out,* Tackle said. *Tell me everything. Your whole day started out with danger! Start at the beginning. Did someone try to kill you this morning?*

*No. I just fell in the water. My own fault. And then I had to go to practice, which was so bad I don't even want to talk about it. But then after practice Ennjy gave me a report. The Tevs and Z-Tevs are making life even worse for Zeenods. Ennjy says we need to find Mehk and get that spybot with evidence from him. I told them Mehk went into hiding on some planet somewhere and that he is expecting me to quit. If he finds out I'm not quitting, he'll be furious. It's all impossible, Tackle!*

*I've been patrolling,* Tackle said. *Somebody was prowling around in front of your house. Could be an assassin. You've got to unlatch this gate before you go to sleep so I can get in and out if I need to. The Pattersons put a new lock on it.*

22

They both froze as they heard Albert's patio door open.

"Albert?" Nana's voice called out. And then through the slats in the fence they could see her walk into the yard.

Albert stood. "Hey, Nana. I'm over here."

"Thought you might be saying hello to Tackle. Hiya, handsome!" She held her hand between two fence slats, and Tackle trotted over and licked it happily.

If Nana were a dog, Tackle thought, she'd be queen of the hood.

"Feeling okay? Have a good nap?" she asked Albert.

"Better, thanks," Albert said.

"Well, I think everybody at school is worried about you. The principal and the nurse and your biology teacher and Mr. Sam all called. Told me the whole story. And I heard your phone go *ping ping ping* about twenty times. I think you have a lot of texts to read, kiddo."

"I'll be right in," Albert said. He whispered a promise to Tackle that he would unlatch his gate later, and then he went over to his own house.

Twenty-three texts. He sat on his bed and scrolled through them. Trey's was first.

*Thought you were dead, Albert. Glad you're not. But you freaking gave me a heart attack.*

Albert had never had so many messages at once. He wasn't sure if he should feel flattered or embarrassed. Up until this moment, he hadn't exchanged many numbers with classmates, so most of the messages were from phone numbers of classmates that he hadn't yet entered as contacts into his phone.

Quickly, he shot off replies to each text, trying to guess who was writing by what they had to say. A whole series basically had the same question, *Are you okay?*

He texted back—either *Yeah thanks!* or *All good!*—a whole bunch of times and then set down his phone. His brain had that overfull feeling, like too many thoughts were firing at once. Partly it was the time-folding. So much had happened to him, and yet not that much Earth time had passed. It was only lunchtime here and already he had fallen into the Patuxent River, failed the gryther test on Gaböq, and heard from Tackle that someone new was lurking around. On top of today's worries was the overall worry that if he and the Zeenods couldn't find Mehk and get that evidence, they'd never be able to free his coach Kayko and the other innocent Zeenods from prison.

And then his phone went crazy. A whole bunch of new messages. He read the first one, which, again, was from Trey.

*Min said she just texted you to see if you wanted to go to Gabby's party with her and you texted back yes. Dude! Freddy likes Min. I thought you liked Jessica?*

Albert's stomach dropped. Gabby's text followed.

*Wow, Albert. Unexpected! Min is cool. I didn't know you liked each other. My party's gonna rock.*

Then Freddy's:

*Albert!!! I thought you were my friend!!!! How could you do this?*

Albert's hands started shaking. He hadn't even realized that Min had texted about the party. He must have texted yes by mistake. It was such a basic shawble—to act while distracted! Stupid! Stupid! Stupid! This was not what he needed right now. And since when did Min like him, he wondered? He was sure she liked Freddy.

He crawled into bed and pulled the covers over his head.

# 1.6

Just before midnight Tackle was pacing, his breath appearing in cloudy puffs. The night was chilly and dry, and the quarter-moon looked like a splintered bone that had been flung up to the sky. He had been patrolling for hours, going in now and then to warm up and lap up a little water, and then slipping back out his dog door to keep watch outside.

He trotted to the gate to make sure it was still unlatched, even though he had seen Albert sneak over and unlatch it less than an hour ago. Yep. Closed, not latched. Then he trotted over to the fence by Albert's house. Still no snow, but the January cold had turned the grass stiff and crunchy.

Wait—*sniff.* Something new. Chicken. *Mmmmm*…Definitely chicken. His ears pricked.

A sound from a distance. Something shuffling…or rolling…It was growing louder. Something was approaching. He ran around to the front, pushed open the gate with his nose, and crept out.

Approaching on the sidewalk was that same shadowy figure he had seen earlier, pulling that wheeled trash can.

*Sniff.* Chicken? He definitely smelled chicken, but he hadn't smelled chicken when he saw this guy before. *Grrrrr.* He tensed to attack, but then the figure stopped and flung a bag toward Tackle. The delicious chicken aroma intensified as the bag sailed over Tackle's head. *Yuuuuuum!* In the Pattersons' yard, the bag exploded. Tackle raced toward it and began tearing into it. A whole roasted chicken! *Yum!*

After a few bites, Tackle realized it could be a trick. He turned around to see the guy running down Albert's driveway into Albert's backyard, pulling his can along. *Grrrr.*

Tackle chased after him, calling out as he passed Albert's bedroom window: *Albert! Intruder!*

Before Tackle could stop him, the guy slipped into the Kinneys' gardening shed, dragging his can in after him, and slammed the door shut.

BAM! Tackle pounced on the door.

Albert raced outside, shuffling awkwardly in his nana's slippers, which were the first things he could grab to put on. *What's going on?*

*I think the guy has a bomb!* Tackle said, keeping up his front paws on the door. *Maybe a huge one.*

With wide eyes, the dog and Albert stared at each other for a moment. *Robot or life-form?* Albert asked. He couldn't believe how badly this day was going, how over-the-top stressful his life was. Just when normal people would be drifting off to dreamland, here he was dealing with an assassin hiding in his shed.

A loud thump sounded against the door, as if the creature inside was trying to get out. Quickly Albert joined Tackle, throwing his weight against the door.

*Give up. We got you!* Tackle said, and then, realizing that who-ever was inside probably didn't understand Dog, he growled. Everybody could understand that.

The movement inside the shed went quiet. Then came the sound of someone muttering. "I risked my life to steal that chicken. I'm starved. I should have just eaten it myself. I hate that dog!"

Both Albert and Tackle recognized the voice and Zeenod lan-guage. *It's Mehk!* Albert whispered.

*He hates me?* Tackle's ears flattened. *Grrrrr. I hate him more.*

"Mehk," Albert said. "We know you're in there. Tackle is strong and capable of ripping you to shreds."

Proud, Tackle thumped on the door and threw in an extra growl.

"It was supposed to be a simple robbery!" Mehk's tone was sharp. "My Z-da is gone. I need yours to get back to my ITV."

"You need me?" Albert said, still bracing against the door. His mind began to whirl. Surely he could use this to his advantage.

Silence, and then a huff from behind the door. "I don't need you," Mehk said. "I need your Z-da to get supplies in my ITV. I have a few minor repairs to make before my creation will be ready to take your place as alternate Star Striker."

*He doesn't know you lied about quitting, Albert!* Tackle said. *Tell him you'll let him make those repairs, but instead hand him over and let Lat and the Tevs take care of him!*

*Ha! I heard that!* Mehk called out in Dog. *I updated my language-translation implant and can understand you now.*

Tackle winced.

But an unexpected calm came over Albert. The Zeenods needed Mehk, and Mehk was here. All Albert had to do was find a way to work with him. "No more lies, Mehk," he said. "I'm going to open this door and we're going to talk about this."

27

*Don't open the door!* Tackle yelped.

*If Mehk had a weapon,* Albert said loud enough for Mehk to hear, *he would have fired it by now.* Albert wasn't sure that was true, but he hoped so.

Silence.

Summoning his courage, Albert motioned for Tackle to back off, and then he opened the door. He expected to see the Zeenod botmaker standing tall with his usual menacing sneer, but instead a crazy-looking guy covered up in a ripped parka and dirty old ski mask was gripping a garbage can.

Tackle snarled, showing his teeth to keep Mehk in his place.

"What's in the can?" Albert asked.

Reluctantly, Mehk dragged out the can and lifted the lid. The sight of a mangled robot with Trey's face sent chills through Tackle's haunches and down Albert's spine.

"Your creation," Albert said, fascinated to see again the robot that he had truly believed was Trey Patterson. "It's completely destroyed! But it was amazing."

"It was perfection." The botmaker straightened up and then glared at Tackle. *And it was destroyed by you!*

*Self-defense!* Tackle cried out. *The thing was attacking me. I had no choice.*

*If it was attacking, it was malfunctioning.* The botmaker scowled. *And the only reason it malfunctioned was because I was thrown into prison and couldn't monitor its systems!* He pulled off his ski mask and took off his parka and threw them on the floor of the shed in disgust.

"Mehk, I know you want to repair it, and I'm sure I would feel the same," Albert said, trying to calm things down. "But we need your help. We need the evidence you collected on your spybot that proves the crimes that Lat—"

"Ha! You think you can take that evidence to the authorities and build a case against Lat and Tescorick?" Mehk laughed. "That will never work. The Tev leadership will deny everything. They'll say you created that evidence."

Albert remembered how Lat had created false evidence to put Kayko in prison. "Maybe," Albert nodded. "But we can't just sit back and give up. You were in prison, Mehk! You know that the Zeenods in prison are innocent. Come with us to Zhidor, bring your spybot and present that evidence—"

"And get thrown back into prison?" Mehk screeched. "No! One Zeenod and one Earthling are not enough to take on all the Tevs and Z-tevs. They want both of us dead, Kinney. They'd find us before we even got to Zhidor."

*Grrrr.* Tackle's muscles tensed.

Albert took a breath. *Mehk's right,* he said to the dog.

"Of course I'm right," the botmaker said. "Even if we did make it to Zhidor, and even if we did present the evidence, the Tevs and Z-Tevs would never open up the prison doors and just let the Zeenods go free."

Mehk's bem stirred, and Albert looked at him, really looked at him. There was a Zeenod standing in his shed with large eyes and skin that swirled with luminous shades of greens and browns and with a beautiful capelike bem attached to his shoulders. He had committed crimes, yes, but he was a Zeenod, and he had been mistreated by the Tevs and Z-Tevs and had been betrayed by his own president. He was a Zeenod whose parents had been killed in prison for speaking out against the occupying aliens that stole their planet. He was also a genius whose inventions had been stolen and who wanted the chance to show the universe what he could do.

"Aren't you tired of this?" Albert asked. "Look at you. You're stuck here. You're homeless. You're hungry. You can't go back to the Fŭigor Solar System. And you won't survive here on Earth. If you help your fellow Zeenods get your planet back, I'm sure whatever crimes you have committed will be forgiven. You and Kayko could work together. You could have everything you need to make those superior robotics that you've wanted to make, not to harm, but to help! You could use your brain to figure out how to reverse the damage to the planet that the Tevs and Z-Tevs have done! You could become the leader you were meant to be. You could become a leader on the free planet Zeeno."

Mehk's bem stirred and his eyes flashed. Albert knew he was listening.

"We need to be on the same team, Mehk," Albert went on. "The first step is to take the spybot with the new evidence about Lat trying to kill me to Zhidor. It's worth trying. You said it yourself—Lat and the Tevs and Z-Tevs are looking for you. If they find you and kill you, the evidence will be gone for good. Let me help protect you and the evidence."

"If you want to take the spybot on a fool's errand to Zhidor, I'll give it to you," Mehk said. "The spybot is in my ITV. Let me go and I'll—"

*It's a trick,* Tackle said, ears flattening. *Couldn't he just fly away if you beamed him up or does he need a Z-da for that?*

*Good point. He wouldn't need a Z-da to pilot the ITV. A Z-da is just for beaming and communication.* He turned to Mehk. "I'll go up with you. Once you give me the spybot, we'll talk about next steps for you."

*Wait,* Tackle barked. *It's too dangerous. Send me.*

Albert stopped and gave his loyal friend a long look.

Tackle nodded. *Send me. You keep his robot down here. Mehk only gets it back if he helps us.* He turned to Mehk and growled. *Hear that?*

"You know that Lat and the Tevs might have discovered my ITV," Mehk said. "They could be waiting. If we go, the dog had better be ready to attack or we could both end up dead."

Keeping one eye on Mehk, Albert took Tackle aside. *He's right. Maybe this is too dangerous,* Albert whispered.

Tackle shook out his muscles. *You need the evidence. Let's get this over with.*

Albert crouched down and gave his friend and partner a hug. *Send me a signal when you have the spybot and I'll beam you back down.*

Tackle nodded.

*Let's have a secret code,* Albert whispered, *in case you have to get a message to me. That way I'll know it's really you giving me the message.* Albert thought back to the time he and Tackle first realized they could communicate, when Albert had given Tackle a carrot. *Say "May this carrot bring you joy,"* Albert whispered. *That will be our secret code.*

*Got it,* Tackle whispered.

They returned to Mehk.

"Okay, Tackle is going with you. Get the spybot and contact me immediately. This should be quick. And Mehk—I love this dog. If you try anything that puts him in danger, you will regret it."

"All I want to do is restore my robot," Mehk said flatly.

Trying to hide the fact that his hands were shaking, Albert programmed the coordinates and then put his Z-da to his lips and activated the szoŭ.

After they disappeared, Albert stood still for a long moment looking at the night sky. The canvas of black with its dotted stars and curved moon looked beautiful and calm, like a painting from a little kid's bedtime book. Come home safely, Tackle, Albert thought, hoping he had done the right thing.

What he couldn't see hovering near Mehk's spacecraft was the ITV piloted by a Tev assassin.

# 1.7

As soon as Tackle and Mehk arrived in the empty ITV, both breathed a sigh of relief.

*All clear. Get the spybot and let's go,* the dog said.

Mehk's mind was spinning. He looked around the spacecraft, trying to find a way to stall so he could think of a next step that worked for him. He certainly had no desire to go back to Earth.

*What are you waiting for?* Tackle barked.

*I can't remember where I put it,* Mehk said, beginning to pace. *Think, think, think. I know I was trying to be clever in hiding it, which means I would have put it somewhere unlik—*

*Stop talking and find it,* Tackle huffed.

*Why don't you stop talking and do something useful?* Mehk huffed in return. *Use that nose of yours and sniff around for explosives. Someone might have found this vehicle and planted a bomb or a surveillance device in it. By the way, never tell me to stop talking. I do better when*

32

*I think out loud. You should be encouraging. Just say, "Believe in your brilliance. You will succeed."*

*No,* Tackle said.

Mehk gave him a withering look. *Well, I'm not impressed with your companionship. I thought you were supposed to be a best friend to whomever you're with. Fine, I'll say it to myself. Believe in your brilliance, Mehk. You will succeed in finding this little spybot that Albert Kinney foolishly thinks will help the entire solar system understand Zeeno's plight.*

*Grrrrrr.* Tackle glared at him. *Keep looking.*

Mehk opened a storage cupboard. The botmaker knew the spybot was inside. He had hidden it under a yit in the back of the cabinet, and he could see now that it was still there. No hurry revealing it, he thought to himself, as he closed the door and opened another cabinet.

*This is taking too long,* Tackle said.

Mehk smiled. *You aren't helping! I miss my gheet. I made the most perfect animatronic pet. It was a gheet—you know, like your Earth tarantula. My gheet knew how to be—*

An alarm interrupted, and Mehk's smile dropped. A large communication screen lit up and a young Tev's face appeared on the screen. Mehk and Tackle froze.

The Tev, surprised to see them, too, cried out, "Whoa!" And the red cigar she had been smoking fell into her lap. "I can't believe this!" She fumbled to put out the cigar and then laughed and jumped up with nervous excitement. "I got you! And the dog, too! Woo-hoo!"

Tackle lunged at the screen and barked, and Mehk sat at the control panel and tried activating the thruster.

At the same time, the Tev uncloaked her vehicle. There it was—a Tev police vehicle in close range.

The Tev leaned into her camera and laughed again, so forcefully that a spray of spit hit the lens. "I never thought I'd be on duty when you came!" She made a call, her gaze shifting to the right. "Madam President, this is Officer Rik. The target is here! He's in his ITV! Kinney's dog is here, too. Even better, right?" Her eyes snapped back to face Mehk. "Hey, botmaker, no use trying to escape! We locked your controls!" She laughed again. "You should see him, Madam President. He's trying to activate manual override and—"

"Patch me in!" the second voice said, and suddenly President Telda Lat's face appeared in a split screen.

"Lat," Mehk said.

The Zeenod president looked relieved to see him. "I thought you might have been insane enough to hide on Earth," she said.

"Yes, you have found me." Mehk's fingers kept tap dancing on the keyboard.

The young officer laughed. "You can't escape! I told—"

"Rik, stop laughing and focus." President Lat's voice was stern. "Do your job. Activate the DRED sensors."

The officer's face fell. "Yes, right! I apologize." She turned away from the screen and began punching a code into her computer system. Her excitement had morphed into anxiety, and they could all hear her whispering instructions to herself.

Lat leaned in. "You know I admire you, Mehk, but I have orders."

"From President Tescorick?"

"Of course."

As he stared at the video screen, Tackle's muscles went rigid. *What's she doing, Mehk?* But he knew. She was preparing to fire a missile.

# 1.8

Albert was shivering in the backyard, staring up at the night sky. The entire mission shouldn't have taken long. And with time-folding, they should have been back already. He realized he should check his phone. Emergency messages from the Zeenods usually came through a high-tech feature on his phone as texts, and he remembered that his phone was still sitting on his bedside table.

Just when he turned to go in, he heard the sound of the Pattersons' back door opening. "Tackle?" Trey called out.

Albert froze, but from Trey's vantage point on his back porch, Trey could see the top of Albert's head over the fence.

"Albert? What are you doing? It's late. Have you seen Tackle?"

"Um—hey. Tackle? No, I haven't." Albert felt horrible lying to his friend, but it was to protect him. "I was just—I thought I heard something. Like a raccoon. We had one a while ago and my mom freaked out. I was just—"

"Tackle?" Trey called out again, walking around the yard. "I was sleeping, and I had another really weird nightmare, and I woke up, and Tackle wasn't inside." He looked over the fence, and then he stopped and shivered. "It's freezing out here. I think he got out again! I don't understand why he's suddenly running away."

"Tackle wouldn't just run away," Albert said. "Um, maybe there was a raccoon and Tackle chased it somewhere."

Trey stopped and looked out toward the front gate, which was open. "Yeah…maybe. I'm telling my dad. He just put a new lock on this. We have to go look for him. Text me if you see him, Albert."

"Sure."

As soon as Trey turned to go inside, Albert raced in to check his phone, careful to be as quiet as possible.

His heart pounded when he saw five messages on his phone. And then he realized that all of them were Earth messages. All of them from Freddy.

*Albert, you went way way way too far. It's bad enough that Min invited you. But you didn't have to say yes.*

*You could have told me to my face that you liked her. Not cool, Albert.*

*Absolutely everybody in the whole school is talking about what a cute couple you and Min are now.*

*I don't think I can look you in the eyes again. Ever.*

*If "Albert" was in the dictionary, I'm sad to say the definition would be "terrible friend."*

Quickly, Albert sent a text back.

*Freddy, I'm sorry. You don't understand. I can explain when I see you.*

The reply was immediate.

*Too late.*

Albert closed his eyes. This was not what he needed.

# 1.9

*This can't be the end.* Tackle shook his head. *There's nothing we can do?*

*Wait for it,* Mehk said.

And then through the video they could hear the Tev's computer announce, "DRED sensors cannot locate the ITV. No smartskin coating is detected."

"Ha!" Mehk grinned, his fingers continuing to fly over the keys. "Madam President, as I'm sure you know, DREDs are programmed to lock onto the chemical signature of the smartskin coating of ITVs, but after I escaped from prison, I deliberately drove through a R'tinuk sandstorm. Sanded all the coating right off."

Lat's eyes went gray and she screamed at the officer. "You didn't test the DREDs upon arrival? What have you been doing?"

The officer began to stammer another apology, and Lat shouted. "Idiot! Well, he can't move, can he? So aim manually and fire!"

"But I'm in blast range, Commander. I need to back up and fire from a safe—"

"Aim, now! And fire at my command. That's an order."

Tackle began running around the small ITV. *Where's the escape pod?*

*There is no pod,* Mehk said, focusing on the controls.

Lat's voice came next. "Aim the DRED!"

The young officer's voice cracked. "Aiming the DRED."

The alarm in Mehk's ITV went off. "Warning. Code 8X. DRED detected in proximity. If launched from current coordinates, complete destruction in ten seconds."

Tackle stopped running.

"Any last words?" Lat asked.

"Go suck on a cigar!" Mehk said.

As Lat issued the command to fire, Mehk pulled a lever and turned the wheel sharply to the right, and the ITV blasted off.

Tackle went flying and thumped against the ITV's side wall.

*Ha!* Mehk cried as they zoomed out of the path of the incoming DRED and flew by the Tev's ITV. *I had thought they might try to lock the controls, so I coded a secret back door for manual override before I left for Earth!*

Tackle regained his balance. *We're alive? You're a genius!*

*They'll try to follow us, but we can outsmart them.* Mehk increased the speed.

Thrilled, Tackle ran to the rear window. Already, the other ITV was just a dot in the distance.

# 1.10

Albert's phone vibrated. A special alert.

*Mehk here. Lat tried to kill us. Must flee. Returning to Earth no longer possible. This is the only way for me and your dog to survive. Too dangerous to send more messages. We will contact you again only when safe. I know you may think this is a trick, but it is true. Your dog said that you would believe it if I added "May this carrot bring you joy."*

Albert stared at the screen. Tackle and Mehk in a chase for their lives? No, no, no!

Outside, he heard the sound of the Pattersons' car starting. Trey and his dad were leaving to drive around the neighborhood in search of a dog that was, at this moment, rocketing through space.

There was a soft knock on the door, and his nana whispered, "Albert?"

Overwhelmed, he set down his phone and told her to come in.

"I saw a crack of light under your door. What's up?" Her long silvery hair was down, and her round face, which was often flushed with pink, was pale. In her white nightgown, she looked like a ghost.

When he tried to tell her he was okay, what came out was a choked and garbled mess.

"Take a breath," she said, sitting on the edge of the bed. "Start again."

Albert inhaled and exhaled. Keeping so much inside was killing him, but he had to be careful not to reveal anything. "I'm just worried because Tackle got out again," he managed to say. "I heard Trey outside calling for him. I think he and his dad just drove off to look for him."

"Oh dear," Nana said. "Tackle has been getting out a lot lately."

Albert hesitated. He wanted to confess that Tackle was with a Zeenod botmaker and that he was never coming back and it was all his fault. "This—this is bad" was all he managed to stammer.

Nana nodded. "In cases like these, I try to remind myself not to assume the worst. Assuming the worst is like feeding a beast that lives in the future. What do we actually know right now? We know that Tackle is smart and strong. Chances are he'll be okay."

"But he's—I—" Albert couldn't finish.

"This is more than Tackle getting out," Nana said. "I can tell. Especially tough day?"

"Nana." He choked up again. "You have no idea."

"Spill the beans, kiddo."

Desperate to unload some of the emotion that was paralyzing him, Albert opened his mouth, and what came out was the only piece of today's disaster he could reveal. "I—I—this is going to sound stupid because I know it's not really important, but today I found out that a girl named Min likes me," he stammered. "She asked me to a Valentine's Day party."

Nana's concerned face broke into a smile. "Well, that sounds like a good thing."

"No. She's not supposed to like me. She's supposed to like Freddy Mills. But I got mixed up and said yes to her and now Freddy is furious. I know. The whole thing sounds like a stupid TV show."

But Nana didn't laugh. "That sounds like a challenge," she said. "When a big thing like a conflict with a friend happens, it's best not to ignore it or shove it down. Just try to think of one positive step you can take to resolve the conflict. Sometimes misunderstandings are easier to iron out than you assume."

*Respond to challenges in positive ways.* That was the last lesson Kayko had recorded for Albert. His mind snapped back to Tackle and Mehk, and he hardly heard his nana remind him that he could come and talk to her anytime. He forced his attention back and said he just needed sleep.

"You got it, kiddo," she said. "Sweet dreams."

As she walked out the door, he was suddenly struck by the thought that she was going to return to her home in New Zealand soon. End of May, she had said. He saw his life stretch out without Nana and without Tackle. Bleak. Sad. And if he and the Zeenods lost the tournament…how could he ever feel good about anything?

As soon as she was gone, he sent a message to Mehk.

*Go to Zhidor, Mehk! It will be the safest place to land. You and Tackle have to stay safe. Then you can get the spybot with the evidence to the Zhidorian authorities.*

Albert waited. And waited. No reply.

Fearing the worst, he sent Ennjy a message explaining what had happened and apologizing for having messed up. Her reply, he knew, was supposed to help him feel better.

*Albert, we will alert our allies to what's happening, and we will talk more on Gaböq at our next practice. You were trying to get the evidence back. I would have taken the same risk.*

But that was just it. Albert had risked nothing. He had sent Tackle to take that risk.

# 1.11

Tackle didn't move. Outside the rear window, he kept expecting to see enemy lights. *I'm happy we're alive. But the chase isn't over. Lat must be furious. What does Albert say?*

41

As Mehk steered the spacecraft, he glanced at the message Albert had sent and shook his head. *Albert still wants us to go to Zhidor.*

*So, you'll set the course,* Tackle said.

*That's exactly where Lat and the Tevs will assume we're going.*

Tackle shook his head. *If Albert says Zhidor, we go to Zhidor.*

*I'm setting a course to zigzag through the Ceejek Space Warp Tunnel,* Mehk said. *It doesn't lead to Zhidor and will be hard for any police vehicles to predict.*

*But*—the dog protested.

*Shhh! Let me think.* The botmaker stood up and began to pace. *We shouldn't be running from the Tevs and Z-Tevs. They are the criminals and the thieves. My whole life I have been forced to work for them. They have taken everything from me. They are the ones who should be running from us.*

*Exactly!* Tackle yelped. *Let's go to Zhidor and get help so we can stop them.*

*No. Even if we got there safely, it would be my word against Lat and the Tev leadership.*

*But,* Tackle said, *you have the spybot with the evidence!*

Mehk walked over to the storage cupboard, pulled the spybot from under the yit, and held it up. *Even if we get this to the Zhidorians, the Tevs and Z-Tevs can say that it's fake. They can say that we spliced footage together to make it look like Lat was the one trying to kill Albert. This bit of footage is not the answer to free Kayko or any other Zeenods. We'd need evidence from many different sources. Forget about it.* He put it back in the cupboard. *We have to find a place to hide, and then we can plan revenge and get them where it hurts—*

Tackle pressed into the floor firmly with all four of his paws, standing tall and lifting his chin. *We are not born to hide. We are not born to hurt. We are born to help. If not with that evidence, then with another kind of action.*

Mehk spun around and stared at Tackle. The dog's face was remarkable, really. Those noble brown eyes and the solemn wrinkles on his forehead. Somehow, Mehk could see the loyalty and love for Albert in the dog's face, and it gave Mehk's heart a squeeze. He thought of his beloved gheet and how sad he had felt when the prison medic killed it. And yet what was that gheet? Just an invention of metal and chips. What would it be like, he thought, to be connected to another life-form with the same kind of loyalty and love that Tackle had for Albert and that Albert had for him? The same kind of loyalty that bound the Zeenods? He thought of old Zin, who had known Mehk's parents, and all the Zeenods in prison who were connected with each other and had trusted him and helped him escape. He thought of Kayko and how brilliant she was. He had always been impressed by her. She had managed to accomplish so much with so little. And the Zeenods had all been counting on him to set her free.

An energized silence filled the ITV, and Tackle noticed that Mehk's bem was extending.

*Could I have been playing the wrong game?* Mehk asked himself.

*What?* Tackle asked.

Mehk began to pace. *I have been trying to show the world my genius by tricking them into believing that my robot is a living, breathing johka player. I wanted to fool my enemies. But what if…what if I used my genius in a much much bigger way?*

*I'm not sure where you're going,* Tackle said.

Mehk paced faster, and he repeated the dog's mantra. *We are not born to hide. We are not born to hurt. We are born to help.*

*What are you thinking?* Tackle asked cautiously.

*Albert suggested I use my genius to help set the Zeenods free. Maybe that is not such a terrible idea.*

Amazed, Tackle remained quiet, giving the botmaker time and space to think.

*Here is the issue,* Mehk went on. *The only way to beat the Tevs is with numbers. It can't be just Albert and you and me demanding justice. We need every Zeenod on every planet and all our allies to come forward with evidence and demand justice all at the same time.*

Tackle's brow wrinkled even deeper. *But lots of Zeenods are in prison—*

*Exactly! That's it!* Mehk blinked. *We have to get the Zeenods out. Let's see…a thousand Zeenods are in each prison and there are lots of prisons. Actually, I'm—*

*Wait. You thinking of a prison breakout?*

Mehk nodded.

*Of not just one Zeenod, but a huge number?*

Mehk nodded again. *Yes! All at the exact same time! You just said it yourself. We need another kind of action. Bold action!*

Tackle trotted closer and looked straight into the botmaker's large violet eyes. *You're serious?*

The botmaker straightened. *I have an extraordinary mind. Once I set it to a task, I work until that task is done. As much as I do not want to admit it, Albert is right. I will have no future if the Tevs remain in control of Zeeno. It is in my best interest to use my genius to free Zeeno.*

Tackle knew Albert would be overjoyed to have Mehk working for, not against, the Zeenods. Although the dog wanted nothing more than to return home to Albert and Trey and the comforts of his ordinary life, he knew he had to help. He nodded and said to the botmaker, *Let's do it.*

At that moment, the computer announced their current fuel supply, and Mehk winced. *We'll need a place to refuel and to plot our next steps.*

*I know just the spot,* Tackle said without hesitation. *Gravespace GJ7. Albert and I crashed there right before the Jhaateez game, remember? The crypt keeper's zawg Laika will help us.*

The calm intelligence of the dog sent a tingle of excitement up Mehk's spine. He had always underestimated this dog, and it was time to stop.

# 2.0

The next morning, Albert was beyond anxious. He had received no message from Mehk overnight. They were dead, he assumed. Or alive but furious with him.

That day, school was a nightmare. Between worrying about Tackle and the whole situation with Min, he couldn't concentrate. He either kept checking for texts from Mehk or else kept writing and deleting texts to Freddy, until one of his teachers confiscated his phone. At lunch, he tried to sit down at Freddy's table to talk, but without a word Freddy picked up his tray and moved. And when Albert saw Jessica sitting with Min, he knew he should walk over and try to fix things, but he couldn't get his feet to cooperate. Trey and Raul were sitting with Gabby and Camila, probably talking about the party, and he couldn't face that, either, so he slipped out of the cafeteria and spent the period in the library.

After school, Trey begged him to help put up lost-dog posters around their neighborhood, and he couldn't say no. Each poster had a photo of Tackle, and every time Albert saw the dog's face he wanted to scream and cry at the same time.

He kept thinking about Lat and wondering how, as a Zeenod, she could be working against Zeeno. To think that she was hunting down the ITV that held Tackle made him feel sick. The desire to get Tackle back, to expose Lat and Tescorick, and to return Zeeno to the Zeenods sent fierce and furious energy to every cell in his body.

On top of everything was fear about training for the game against the Gaböqs.

On Wednesday morning he sent a message to Ennjy.

*I can't play on Gaböq. It's not just the grythers. I should've told you. All my life I've been afraid of swimming. I can't deal with the eels and my fear of drowning at the same time. There's no way I can come to practice. I think I need to quit.*

As soon as he sent it, he expected to feel relieved. But he didn't. He just felt lost.

As he arrived at school, he received a message back, a message that brought a new wave of tension.

*You are our Star Striker, Albert. Come to practice. We will talk.*

At lunchtime, with a heavy, anxious heart he activated the szoŭ and went to join his teammates on Gaböq.

47

"Albert," Ennjy said. "We are trying to find Mehk's ITV before our enemies do."

"We know you are anxious about Tackle," Toben said. "We want him safely back, too."

The other Zeenods nodded in agreement.

Albert looked at their kind faces. "No offense, but what can you guys do? You can't even leave Zeeno without permission from the Z-Tevs."

"We have managed to get a message to Lightning Lee, who is now communicating with Zeenod refugees who are living on other planets," Giac said. "Everyone is vowing to join the search."

"Hope is growing," Doz added.

"We must focus on our job. Our job is to play our best against the Gaböqs and do nothing to cause our disqualification," Ennjy said. "At the last practice, I made a mistake and should have introduced Albert to the under-river step by step. I am going to take him down now to work on his fears while you all run drills on the field. But first, the ahn ritual."

A hot flash of shame and panic lit Albert's face as they circled up to meditate. Instead of using the time to connect with the ahn, he spent the time telling himself what a failure he was. The next thing he knew, he was following Ennjy to the end of the field.

"I'm—I'm sorry, Ennjy. It's stupid for me to be so afraid, but I can't—"

"Fear is natural, Albert. Your brain sees or feels danger and tells your body to flee. That is a smart reaction. The trick is not to make fear go away, but to learn to manage it. Acknowledge the fear without judgment. That's the first step."

"Kayko tried to teach me that," Albert said ruefully.

Ennjy nodded. "So we'll practice." On the ground behind the goal, she crouched down and opened a round hatch—like a sewer cover. This was the same one that Doz had helped Albert climb out of after the last disaster. The Gaböq players rarely needed an escape hatch, but regulation required one in every practice facility and stadium.

"We are going down together," Ennjy said. "And we'll get into the river slowly together."

As the aroma of the cold, dark cavern wafted up, the memory of Albert's last experience came with it, turning the muscles in his knees to liquid.

Ennjy's smartfabric uniform glowed as she descended, illuminating the ladder that went straight down. Albert told himself to follow her, but he couldn't. "Ennjy...?" Albert's voice trailed off.

Ennjy stopped and looked up.

"I've been thinking," Albert went on. "During halftime at the very first game, Lee said I could either be a help or a hindrance to the team. Maybe I should sit out this game even if it means we'd be down a player. I mean, we don't really even need to win. We've already won two games in the tournament and Tev and Jhaateez have only won one each. We're in the lead. After this game, we'll play against the winner of the Tev and Jhaateez game, right? Isn't that how the tournament works here?"

Ennjy's face softened and she climbed back up. "The Fŭigor tournament is structured so that the two teams who have won the most matches play against each other. Yes, even if we lose against Gaböq, we should go on to play whoever wins the Tev and Jhaateez game. But every game counts. Let's say we play against Gaböq and we are pushed to such a limit, we break a FJT rule. We attack a ref or start a fight—"

"But that wouldn't happen," Albert said.

"You never know," Ennjy said. "If it did happen, we could

become disqualified from the entire tournament and Gaböq would win the match automatically. And then, Gaböq and the loser of the Tev versus Jhaateez game would be tied and a match between them would be added before moving to the final game. It has happened in the past! For every individual and every team, every game is an opportunity to either fail or to grow stronger. Rather than quitting before you try, please try," she said gently. "I'll devote this whole session to you. I've also created some new lessons to transfer to your Z-da. I'm not as wise as Kayko, but I've tried to give you lessons that address my own shawbles and that I know Kayko would want you to practice."

Palms and forehead sweating, Albert forced himself to follow his teammate down. As soon as they were both standing on the narrow bank, she said, "Just stand here with me and connect with the ahn. Breathe with me, but keep your eyes open to take in the beauty." She took his hand. "There is beauty, and it can help to connect with it."

He felt embarrassed to think how childish he must look holding Ennjy's hand. But her hand, still warm from the hot temperature above ground, was comforting, and he didn't want to let go.

He breathed, feeling Ennjy's bem lift and lower slightly with every inhale and exhale. The golden glow from their uniforms reflected off the river and danced on the cavern walls. It was cool and beautiful down here, and if he could be like Doz and relax, he could even see it being enjoyable. He looked around. The cavern was huge, with a series of interconnected rivers gently streaming through its rocky landscape. Some of the under-rivers were narrow, with narrow rocky ledges on either side. Some of the under-rivers were wider. Stalactites and stalagmites formed jagged columns near the edges of the cavern walls. Erin had recently had to do a project on both for her science class, and she had made stalactites and stalagmites out of clay. He could see his family in the kitchen—Nana helping to mix the bakeable clay.

Now that Albert was seeing all the rocks, he wondered why the only threat the Zeenods had warned him about was falling into the eel-infested water. "What if a fissure opens above a spot where there are rocks below? Nobody could survive that."

"Giac could explain it better," Ennjy said. "But fissures only open above water. So no worries there."

Albert supposed he should be thankful for that, at least.

"Repeat after me: My breathing implant will keep my lungs safe. My uniform will keep my body temperature safe. I can remain underwater here for hours and I will not be harmed."

Albert repeated each statement.

"These are not things you can tell yourself once. You will need to keep reminding yourself," she said. "As for the grythers, the more you are in their presence, the less you will react."

She let go of his hand and lowered herself into the water. Keeping one hand on the rocky ledge, she gestured with the other. "Come in slowly. We will stay here by the ledge."

Albert lowered himself in and clung to the ledge with both hands.

Patiently, Ennjy stayed with him until he gradually let go.

"Excellent. You can tread water gently or you can float."

Albert was about to float when he saw a dark shape slithering on the surface of the water toward them. "One's coming!"

"Remain calm and it will pass," Ennjy said.

But Albert grabbed onto the ledge and hoisted himself out, kicking and splashing.

On the ledge, he turned around to see the gryther glide past Ennjy and rush toward the exact spot where he had churned up the water. The eel bumped against the wall a few times and then swam away.

Albert could barely look at Ennjy. "I'm sorry. I'll never get this."

"Albert. There are two whole months until the game! You can get this. Let's try again."

For the entire practice, Albert went in and out of the water, each time lasting a little longer and floating a little farther.

"How did it go?" Doz asked when they surfaced. "We didn't hear any zaps!"

Albert knew he had only taken baby steps, but Ennjy said she was proud of his progress and the entire team pulled in for a group fist bump.

# 2.1

Adrenaline pulsed through Tackle when they landed on Gravespace GJ7. To remain undercover, they had to land on the outskirts and walk—the way he and Albert had done before. And just two minutes in, the haagoolts arrived, flying toward them with their raylike wings in the darkening sky.

*Grrrr.* He could still feel the chomp of that haagoolt jaw on his foot from the last time he and Albert had landed on GJ7. But he stood his ground, inhaled, and let out a great howl before they were even close.

Immediately, the horrible shapes turned and flew away.

*Impressive,* Mehk said with a nod. *Keep it up. We've got a long walk.*

Over the bone-laden ground they walked, and when they neared the first of the crypt keeper's buildings, Laika trotted out.

*Tackle!*

While Mehk stood awkwardly to the side, the dog and zawg greeted each other with delight. As soon as Tackle explained the situation, Laika suggested they use Trey's old hibernation facility as their hideout.

Tackle beamed at Mehk. *Lucky for you, I got charm.*

Mehk followed, and when they were safely inside, Tackle begged Mehk to send a message to Albert so that he wouldn't worry.

*No.* Mehk shook his head. *The more secretive our mission, the more likely we will succeed.*

*What do you need?* Laika asked.

*Time and supplies,* Mehk said. Immediately he began to pace, thinking through various plans out loud. *The prison system depends entirely on the personal security drones called PEERs. Every imprisoned Zeenod is guarded by a PEER. The first step is to gain control of the PEERs. We can't get a PEER control device to give to each Zeenod. So what can we do? Maybe I could change the PEERs' code? What if I could make the PEERs respond to the Zeenods' commands instead of their ordinary protocols?* His energy changed. He smiled broadly. *Not bad! Perhaps I could introduce that code through a virus?*

*Would that work?* Tackle asked, not quite understanding but liking how excited Mehk was getting.

*I can make it work,* Mehk said. *It's brilliant! Brilliant! But I'll need supplies.* He started listing them off, but Laika interrupted.

*Most of what you need isn't in any of the buildings on GJ7. But,* Laika said, *I have an idea.*

Several hours later, when a Tev spacecraft arrived to drop off its load, they were all ready.

Laika distracted the drivers, and Tackle and Mehk snuck on board their vehicle. Tackle guarded the door and Mehk headed straight for their main control room.

*Make it quick,* Tackle said. *And make sure you don't take anything they'll notice right away.* The thought of being caught by these guys sent a chill through the dog. The scent they left behind smelled like a combination of gasoline and vinegar. Nose in air, ears pricked, he waited and waited.

In the next moment, he heard a bark in the distance, a signal from Laika that the Tevs were returning. He turned to get Mehk, and Mehk was already running toward him, his arms full of gear.

They rushed into the shadows just as the Tevs turned the corner.

*Ha!* Mehk whispered. *We're brilliant!*

Tackle shook out the tension. He was homesick for Albert and Trey, but it felt good to be working again.

# 2.2

"It's garbage day tomorrow," Albert's mom said as they were clearing the dinner dishes. "Whose turn is it to take it out?"

"Mine," Erin said.

"I thought I saw the can in the backyard," his mom went on. "Make sure to—"

At that moment Albert realized he hadn't dealt with the dead robot in the garbage outside, and he jumped up. "I'll do it!"

Erin gave him a look. "Why?"

"Random act of kindness!" he said, running into the kitchen to grab the bag. "What can I say? I'm an amazing guy!"

While his mom and Nana and Erin watched with amusement, Albert ran around the house collecting the rest of the garbage, and then he took the bag outside. He threw it in their can, which was at the side of the house, and then ran around to the back and peeked inside the trash can Mehk had left.

Robotic Trey's mangled head stared up at him.

He shuddered, unsure what to do. If his mom or Nana or Erin saw this, they would absolutely freak out. But so would the garbage guys. They'd call the police. Albert would probably be arrested for murder.

He rummaged in the shed and found extra-large, sturdy leaf bags. If he could put the body parts in a bag or two and tie them up tight, they'd get crushed in the truck before anyone saw what was in them. Queasily, he started pulling out parts and putting them in the bag. The skin felt so real, he thought he might throw up. He got the head and torso into one bag and tied it up. Then he started working on the arms and legs. "This is disgusting!" he said to no one in particular.

"Hey, Albert." Trey's voice made him spin around. "I thought I heard you."

"Um. Hi!" Albert cried out, quickly slamming the lid back on the can.

"Somebody just called. They thought they saw Tackle over by the high school. My dad and I are going to go look."

Now guilt added to the tension. Trey and his dad weren't going to find Tackle here on Earth.

"Do you need help? That looks heavy." Trey picked up the bag with the torso and head.

"No!" Albert jumped over and grabbed it from him. "I mean, thanks, but I'm supposed to do this. You know, a chore. It's nice of you to offer, but, you know, my mom would get all crazy if she knew I didn't do it. Moms, right?" He laughed.

Trey gave him a funny look, and as soon as he left, Albert breathed a sigh of relief.

# 3.0

That Thursday at school, Albert had a plan. He wanted to listen to Ennjy's lesson during a morning class, and he wanted to put things right with Freddy at lunch. And then, when he went to his clarinet lesson after school, he wanted to explain to Jessica what had happened with the texts and ask her for advice about how to tell Min he had made a mistake.

But during the morning, he couldn't find a single moment to call up a lesson. That was okay, he told himself. He'd do it tonight.

At lunch, he walked up to Freddy, and Freddy picked up his tray and moved to a new table. This time, Albert followed. "Freddy, I'm going to sit down wherever you are, so just stay there. Please."

Freddy stabbed a chicken nugget and shrugged. "I don't know why you want to sit here. Min is sitting over there."

Albert sat down and leaned in. "Freddy, I've been trying to tell you that I texted yes to Min without knowing what the text was about."

Freddy rolled his eyes. "Give me a break."

"It's true. I thought she was asking if I was all right after falling into the river. I texted back yes. I got a thousand texts from people in a row. I didn't read them carefully."

Freddy set down his fork and stared at Albert. "That sounds like an excuse."

"It's the truth—"

Freddy shook his head. "You're just saying it because I'm mad at you and you don't want to lose me as a friend and that's kind of nice, but not really because—"

"Freddy, you have to believe me. I'm going to tell Min I made a mistake. I'll tell her you—"

Now Freddy leaned in, his eyes full of panic. "Albert, don't you dare!"

"But—"

"Don't say anything!" Freddy blinked, as if his eyes were about to fill up. "She likes you, Albert. She invited you. Not me. There's nothing you could possibly do to make this better. And anything you try will make it worse, so back off and leave me alone. We just need to live our own separate lives now." He picked up his tray, speed-walked to the trash can, dumped his food in, and walked out of the cafeteria.

Albert took a bite of the peanut butter sandwich he had brought from home and then had trouble swallowing it. He looked around the room. Jessica, Min, and Gabby were sitting together by the windows. He wished he could walk over and explain what had happened, but he couldn't stand the thought that Min might feel humiliated and that the others might then be mad at him for hurting her feelings. He felt stuck and didn't have a clue how to get unstuck.

After school, he was too embarrassed to run the risk of seeing Jessica, so he texted his mom and Mr. Sam, telling them he had a bad headache and didn't think he could take his lesson. His mom said to go home and Mr. Sam said he hoped he felt better soon.

Fortunately, when he arrived home the house was empty. He crawled into bed. Again he tried writing texts to Freddy and Jessica and again he kept erasing them. Nothing sounded right.

A disaster of a day.

Holding his phone, he realized he hadn't even found time to listen to Ennjy's meditation. Emotionally wrecked, he sat and called up the audio file.

*Welcome to the seventh lesson: Letting disturbances come and go without reacting. Take a few moments to focus on your breathing and to be present, and we will begin.*

Albert took a breath. Hearing Ennjy's voice helped. He might not have friends on Earth, but he had the Zeenods. Ennjy and Kayko and the team needed him. They needed him to be the best johka player possible against the Gaböqs. That was where he should put his energy. He took another breath and turned his attention back to Ennjy.

*We often experience disturbances. You need quiet and yet there are loud people in your space. Asking people to be* quiet might be a possible solution. In conflicts, learning when to take action is important. But don't forget—one of the most effective actions is, in fact, inaction. Let whatever is bothering you occur without reacting to it. The strongest and the wisest know how to remain calm.

Let whatever is bothering you occur without reacting to it, Albert said to himself. That's not easy.

*When you are in a situation where there is noise or disturbance, such as a busy school hallway or sidewalk, focus on the ahn. Breathe slowly and deeply. Say to yourself: I do not have to react to these disturbances. Imagine you are the calm center of a storm that is raging all around you. Focus on that inner core of calm instead of focusing on whatever is competing for your attention. This is difficult and requires practice, but, with genuine, full-hearted practice, your ability to remain at peace will improve. Take a moment to reflect.*

Albert could definitely relate. He knew that one of his shawbles was to react too quickly to a situation with fear or anger and then regret it later. This would be a good lesson to practice. Even better if he could find a place with annoyances around. As he was about to open his door, Erin walked in, slamming the door against his forehead.

"Erin! Ouch! You're supposed to knock. And you're supposed to be at the gym."

"Sorry. I got sent home. I sprained a tendon or muscle." She hopped in, sat on his bed, and put a bag of ice on her ankle. "You're supposed to be at your clarinet lesson."

"I have a headache. How bad is your ankle?"

"Coach didn't think it needed an X-ray. Nana is getting a phone call from the doctor right now. I have to elevate it."

"Elevate in your room."

"Don't be mean. I just came in here looking for the remote. It's not by the TV."

He was about to tell her to go away when he changed his mind. "You want to play a game?"

"What's the game?"

"I'm trying to improve my concentration. While I sit here, I want you to bother me."

"Like this?" She threw a pillow at him and laughed.

"It's more of a mind game," he said. "Just say stuff or make noises. Try to distract me. I'm going to practice ignoring you. Give me a few seconds to get calm." He sat on the bed and took a deep breath, and then he focused his gaze on the floor.

"This is weird," she said.

"Yeah, well, I'm weird." He breathed again. "Okay. Go for it, Erin."

She waved first with one hand, then with the other, then with both hands. "Yoo-hoo! Look at me, Albert."

He kept still.

She started bouncing on the bed. "Blah-bitty, blah-bitty, blah!" She stopped and made a face.

"I do not have to react to these disturbances," Albert chanted in a soft, even voice.

She laughed and got off the bed, buzzing next to him like a fly, flapping her wings and zooming in close to one ear.

"My inner core is calm," Albert chanted.

"Albert's a doofus," she said. "Goofy, boofy doofus!"

"I am at peace."

"Oh yeah?" Erin started hopping in front of him. "You think you can ignore me? Take this!" She turned around and stuck out her rear end and with an epic noise, pretended to let go of one huge fart.

He laughed.

"Gotcha!" she yelled, and started dancing around.

"Hey," he said, noticing she was jumping on both feet. "I thought you sprained your ankle."

She stopped and her face dropped.

"You're faking it?" Albert asked.

"Don't tell. I just wanted to come home." She sat back on the bed.

"Let me guess. Your friend Brittany said something mean."

"She's not my friend anymore and I don't want to talk about it," Erin said.

"Erin, you and Brittany are on the same gymnastics team. This thing with Brittany is a problem."

"Let's play again. Switch places," she said, ignoring him. "You annoy me this time."

"No way. I need the practice. Do it again for me."

"Let me try, Albert, or I won't do it ever again for you." She stood in the middle of the room and closed her eyes.

Albert sighed. "Okay. Breathe in and out. Tell yourself that nothing I can do or say is worth your attention. Really believe it." He stopped and smiled. "Actually, this is a great exercise for you, Erin. Pretend I'm Brittany, and I'm in your face. Practice letting it all roll off."

She nodded, standing still, her face struggling to compose itself.

Sometimes, how small his sister looked triggered a desire in Albert to protect her. A while ago, she had come back upset from her Winter Invitational gymnastics tournament. Right before the competition, Erin lost a charm that Brittany had given her for good luck. She thought she had lost it through her own carelessness and was seriously upset, but then another girl on the team told Erin that Brittany had deliberately hidden the charm to freak Erin out. Albert was furious. Brittany seemed to be willing to do anything to make sure Erin didn't outperform her. Albert wanted to confront Brittany and tell her to just stop being mean, but there would be more Brittanys. What Erin needed was to learn how to protect herself. The exercise was a good start.

Albert circled Erin and made his voice high-pitched and whiny, like Brittany's. "Hey, Erin, the coach said my routine is the best. I'm going to win all the medals at the next tournament."

Erin's eyes flew open. She turned to Albert, her face turning red. "I hate you, Brittany Marshall, and I hope you get a cow disease!"

"Erin." Albert smiled. "That's reacting. Try it again. This time, tell yourself you don't have to react to any disturbances. Really believe it, because it's true."

Erin nodded.

Albert turned back into Brittany. "Hi, Erin! Did you know that everybody in school loves me and nobody loves you?"

"I do not have to react to any disturbances," Erin said.

"Good!" Albert said. Then he used Brittany's voice again. "Hey, Erin, I got twelve thousand likes on my TikTok video. Everybody thinks I'm soooooo talented!" He started dancing around, and Erin had to force down a tiny smile.

"You are nothing compared to me, Erin!" Albert taunted.

"I can hear you, but I'm not going to care," Erin said.

Albert stopped and smiled. "Erin, that's so good!"

Nana walked in. "Albert! I thought I heard your voice."

"He has a headache," Erin said quickly, hopping on the bed and putting the ice back on her ankle.

"I think it's actually a cow disease," Albert said, and Erin smiled.

Nana looked at them. "A headache and a sprained ankle? What next? Well, now I can ask you both this question. My doctor has been suggesting that I do a little swimming to improve the mobility of this hip. And Erin's doctor just suggested that she should take a couple of weeks off gymnastic practice and do some swimming to improve that ankle of hers. And I was thinking, well, if Erin and I are going to the indoor pool a couple of times a week, maybe all three of us should go."

"Albert hates to swi—" Erin started to say, just as Albert shouted, "Yes!"

Erin and Nana both looked at him, surprised by his enthusiasm. "I do hate to swim," Albert said. "But I was just thinking I should get over it."

Nana smiled. "Excellent. I was dreading going alone, but with all of us going, it'll seem like fun instead of work. Team Kinney!" Nana put out her fist. Albert and Erin smiled and gave her a bump.

# 3.1

*Sniff. Sniff.* Tackle's nose twitched, searching for the smell of gheet eggs. *How many more do we need?* he asked the botmaker.

Mehk looked at the collection of eggs in the mailing container he was holding. *Two or three more nests should do it.*

Tackle poked his head inside a storage room in the crypt they were in and gave another sniff. His ears pricked. Definitely the smell of gheet eggs here. A woody, wormy smell.

*Once I hated your olfactory ability,* Mehk said. *But now I admire it.*

Tackle had to laugh. Under a bottom shelf on the right, the smell was strongest, and, sure enough, after Tackle pointed out the space, Mehk reached under it with a long stick and gently pulled out another soft beige sphere of woven gheet silk, about the size of a Ping-Pong ball. In it, about three hundred gheet eggs were waiting to hatch. Carefully, he added it to the four others in the mailing container.

*Ha! Well done, Tackle.*

Laika joined them. *Gheet hunting? Why?*

Mehk smiled. *These gheet eggs are going to get us into the prison. You'll see! One more and we'll be ready.*

*I'm happy to help get rid of gheets,* Laika said. *Nobody likes gheets.*

*I do!* Mehk cried. *Gheets make wonderful pets.*

Laika looked at Tackle. *Is he kidding?*

*Nope.* Tackle shrugged.

After another nest was found, they returned to their hideout, and Mehk hid the six egg nests in the bottom of a cigar box and covered them with a packing sheet and neatly lined red cigars on top. Next came a note addressed to Blocck, the Z-Tev warden of the prison that Mehk had been in. Mehk read it aloud as he wrote it out.

*In appreciation of your work. Compliments of High Command.*

*Do you think Blocck will try to find out exactly who sent the package?* Tackle asked.

Mehk shook his head. *Blocck will be happy to get free cigars. And now the final touch.* The botmaker plucked the new spybot he had made from old parts and dropped it in the mailing container. *With this, we'll be able to see everything!*

*Once, I hated your spybot-making ability,* Tackle said. *But now I have to admire it.*

Mehk laughed and bowed. He packed the surprise in a shipping container addressed to Blocck, and Laika showed him how to get it on the next transport vehicle.

A warm feeling grew in Mehk's chest, and he looked at both animals. He wasn't sure exactly how to define the feeling, but he had to admit, at least to himself, that it was nice to be part of a team.

# 4.0

As Albert walked to the edge of the diving platform, he imagined he was standing on a Gabōq johka field. The board at this indoor pool was twenty-five feet high—which was a little less than the distance between a fissure and an eel-infested under-river. Excellent practice. This was the sixth time he and Nana and Erin had come since that day in January when they had made their pact to swim.

"Try a flip!" Erin called on the ladder behind him.

"I don't need to flip. I just need to fall," he said, and looked at the clear blue water below. Although he had improved, standing there still made his knees weaken and his stomach hurt. In one of the swim lanes ahead, he could see Nana getting in her laps. She was old, but she was a beast.

"Jump!" Erin said. "I'm getting cold."

Albert jumped. Imagine the water is full of grythers, he told himself. As soon as he sank, he opened his eyes. He was tempted to stay down for a long time but didn't want anybody to get suspicious. Using as little effort as possible, he rose to the surface and then floated on his back.

"You look dead!" Erin called down.

"Thank you. I'm calm," he said.

"Watch me!" Like the gymnast she was, she did a flip off the board and landed in a dive, and then she kicked her way to the top and swam to the floating Albert.

"Do something other than float, Albert. Want me to teach you how to dog-paddle?" She laughed and splashed him.

At the mention of the word *dog,* a deep longing to see Tackle hit Albert. It was possible, he knew, that he might never see Tackle again, and he didn't know how he could handle that.

"I'm going up again," Erin said, treading water next to him. "I love this."

"Why don't you just tell Mom you want to quit gymnastics?" Albert asked.

She didn't say anything, and he turned his head to see her.

"Be honest," he said. "Do you want to quit?"

"I can't."

"Why not?"

"I don't know," she said. "Isn't there anything you should do but for some reason you can't?" She swam away.

Her question made him instantly think about the Valentine's Day party. He had to tell Min that he couldn't go with her. That he had made a mistake. The party was in twelve days, and he had done nothing but avoid the whole mess. *When you're overwhelmed, take one positive step,* his nana had said. *Respond to challenges in positive ways,* Kayko had said. He had tried to tell Freddy what really happened, and Freddy didn't even believe him. And after that, Albert had given up.

His body felt suddenly heavy and tired. He had been training nonstop. On his walks to school, he tried to keep imagining that fissures were opening, and he practiced jumping over and over. At the park, he ran drills, abruptly changing directions when pretending that a fissure was opening up. All this without Tackle to keep him safe and to keep him company. He still had over a month until the game on Tev, and the pressure was intense. And every time he traveled back and forth for practice, there was the risk that he would be kidnapped or shot at or forced to crash.

With sudden determination to at least resolve the Min thing, he hopped out of the pool and walked over to where his backpack was hanging on a hook. An idea was coming to him. He created a group text with Gabby and everybody she'd invited—Freddy, Min, Jessica, Trey, Raul, and the others—and then he sent a message before he could talk himself out of it.

> *Hey everybody. I'm really sorry. I can't go to the party. My sister has a big gymnastics meet and our whole family is going.*

It was a lie. And it only accomplished one thing: it gave him an excuse for not going with Min. He still had to find a way to explain the truth to Jessica and to convince Freddy that he really hadn't intended to say yes to Min.

# 4.1

*Yes!* Mehk cried out.

Tackle roused from his nap on one of the crypt hibernation tables and looked up.

Mehk was watching the screen of a small computer he had stolen from the Tev spacecraft. On the screen he had a view of Blocck and his office. *Look! Blocck opened the mailing container! The spybot is activated.*

Tackle trotted over and looked at the streaming footage. The tiny spybot Mehk had sent along with the cigars had already flown up and attached to the ceiling, giving Mehk and Tackle a view of what was happening.

Blocck's meaty hands pulled the cigar box out of the mailing container. With a grunt he opened the box and withdrew a red cigar to inspect it. With another approving grunt, he lit it and took a puff.

Mehk laughed and laughed. *My idea is working! Soon the place will be crawling with gheets!*

*And remind me why that's so important,* Tackle said.

Mehk just smiled. *You'll see.*

# 5.0

On Sunday, by the time he and Nana and Erin got home from the swimming pool, Albert had a text from Freddy.

*Min just texted me. After she got your text, she texted me. She asked me to the party and I said yes! And there's something hilarious. She told me she got our phone numbers mixed up! When she sent you the text about the party, she thought she was sending me the message! When you said yes back she thought it would hurt your feelings if she told you she had made a mistake. Hahahahaha lol. Right?*

Albert laughed out loud. He couldn't believe it. The whole big mess was just a whole big misunderstanding. And then he felt a tiny pang of…what? Disappointment? Hurt? Even though he liked Jessica, he realized that it had felt nice to think that Min liked him. Albert caught himself. Really, it was great that Min liked Freddy. It was more than great. Perfect. Another text from Freddy popped up.

*I'm not mad anymore. Are you mad at me?*

Albert smiled and texted back.

*All good.*

Another message popped up.

*There's another funny thing. Gabby's parents canceled their thing for that night so Gabby had to ask them if she could have a party. Her mom said she could have friends over but only if it wasn't a date thing. So basically, we're all just going by ourselves anyway. Hahahahaha lol.*

Albert was struck with a much bigger pang of disappointment. Now that it wasn't a couples party, it was probably going to be fun, and he was going to miss out. If he hadn't lied about having to go to a gymnastics meet, he could have gone. As Tackle would say, *Grrrrr.*

But there was still one problem. Jessica still didn't know the whole truth and probably still thought Albert liked Min instead of her. He had to figure out a way to let her know, and made a vow to talk to her before or after his music lesson on Thursday.

That week, he threw himself into training. But on Thursday after school, Jessica seemed to have disappeared. He didn't see her walking home from school and she wasn't at her house when he got there.

While he was sitting in the living room waiting for the student before him to finish, he remembered that he had another of Ennjy's ahn lessons to do. Getting comfortable, he plugged his earbuds in, called up the audio program, and closed his eyes.

*Welcome to the eighth lesson: Avoiding assumptions. Take a few moments to focus on your breathing and to be present, and we will begin.*

Albert took a deep breath in, let it out, and thought about the topic. Making assumptions wasn't really one of his shawbles, so he wasn't sure how helpful this lesson was going to be. Ennjy should probably have given him a lesson about lying! That would be on target.

*Making assumptions about ourselves or others can cause problems. Yet often we don't even realize we are making an assumption. To do this meditation, first think of someone you know. Next, think or write down some things that you assume about this person. They can be big or small issues.*

Albert thought of Jessica. He assumed she didn't like him anymore.

*Now, turn those assumptions into questions and ask the person you were thinking about those questions directly. After you have received the answers, take a moment to reflect.*

*Ding!* The bell signaled the end of the lesson. Ask questions directly? What? No way. If he was going to do this, he had to do it with someone easier. He pulled out his notebook. Someone safe.

Mr. Sam. He wrote down the first two assumptions that came to mind in his notebook.

1. *I assume Mr. Sam wants Jessica to love music as much as he does.*
2. *I assume Mr. Sam and his wife like to go to concerts.*

He was about to write down another assumption when the student Mr. Sam had been teaching came out, and it was Albert's turn.

"Hey, Albert!" Mr. Sam waved him into the little music room. "Missed you last time. How's it going?"

"Good." Albert sat down and took his clarinet out. "Hey. I—I was just wondering. I mean, I was just listening to this thing about families and jobs and stuff and I was wondering. Do you want Jessica to, like, become a musician?"

"Actually, I don't think music is Jessica's thing," Mr. Sam said. "She plays really well, but I would be surprised if she chose music. She might choose art. Have you seen her sketchbook?"

Albert nodded. "She draws in class all the time and everything she draws is amazing. But…does that make you sad? I mean… because music such a big part of your life?"

Mr. Sam shrugged. "Nope. My dad wanted me to be a vet. Not my thing. I promised myself I'd never pressure my kid. What about your dad? Does he want you to follow in his footsteps?"

"My dad died when I was little."

Mr. Sam winced. "Oh, sorry. I knew that."

"What about your wife?" Albert asked. "Does she feel the same way you do?"

Mr. Sam gave him a funny smile. "Well, I don't have a wife. In fact, I've never been married."

Albert felt his face get hot. "I—I assumed—"

"It's okay. Families come in all sizes and shapes. Jessica's mom and I were dating when we found out a baby was coming. We were going to get married, but after a few months we discovered we were not a good fit. Jessica's mom wasn't ready for marriage, but I was older and ready. When Jessica was just two, her mom decided it would be best for Jessica to give me full custody." He stopped. "You know, since you and Jessica are friends, I should probably ask her how she feels about me talking about this."

"I'm sorry. I didn't mean—we can totally drop it. The whole thing was just...it's just not important."

They both turned their attention to the music lesson, but Albert kept thinking. Wow. That was two assumptions for two that he had gotten wrong. He wasn't sure how Ennjy wanted him to connect all this with johka, but he knew she had her reasons.

# 5.1

Mehk was ready. Every day he had been checking the spybot footage, and finally he saw the exact scenario he was hoping for. Those six hidden nests of gheet eggs had hatched. That meant about eighteen hundred tiny gheets had emerged from Blocck's cigar box and were crawling around Blocck's office. Now Mehk was watching footage of the furious warden as he ran around trying to squish the gheets.

*You're happy but you're wincing,* Tackle said to Mehk as he watched the scene with him.

*I would never kill a gheet. I like gheets,* Mehk said.

Tackle smiled. *You have a heart, Mehk.*

Mehk threw him a look. *If you mean I have an internal organ that serves to pump blood through my arteries and veins, then yes.*

Blocck's frustrated scream pulled their attention back to the video.

*Come on, Blocck,* Mehk said. *Make the call!*

Seconds later, Blocck yelled at his assistant. "Call the exterminator!"

*Ha!* Mehk cried, preparing his stolen laptop to intercept the call.

Tackle watched and listened as Mehk patched in, pretending to be an exterminator, and arranged a date to come.

*We're in,* Mehk said.

*We?* Tackle asked.

*You're coming with me,* Mehk said. *The Zeenods in prison know me as a traitor. I'll need your help to convince them that I'm working for them, not against them.*

Tackle's brow wrinkled. *But you do know I'm famous? Everyone in the Füigor Solar System knows what I look like.*

*I'm famous, too,* Mehk said. *That's why we're both going in disguise.*

# 6.0

On the evening of February 14, Valentine's Day, Albert found himself alone. Erin was at Brittany's, his mom was at another meeting, and everyone else in the world was at Gabby's party. Even Nana was occupied. She was in her room, but she was doing a whole series of video calls with the staff that was running her school back in New Zealand. Frequently, Albert forgot that his nana wasn't just a nana, she was also the founder of a little nature-education school back in New Zealand, which was where she usually lived, and she had online meetings that kept her busy.

After eating an entire bag of chips, watching bad TV, and feeling sorry for himself, he grabbed his coat, texted Nana that he was going for a walk, and took off for the park. It was only seven o'clock. He figured getting out of the house would make him feel better, but he couldn't shake his blues. Gabby's party was just starting, and although he tried not to think about it, he kept imagining his friends laughing and having fun without him. To make matters worse, he passed dog walker after dog walker, which just made him miss Tackle more and more. Nothing was going to get solved. Tackle would never come home and the Zeenods would never break free. And everything he had been doing, all the risks, all the training, was all for nothing.

Once he was at the park, he took the path to the pond and walked all the way to the edge of the dock. The wintry air was cold, but not cold enough to freeze the pond. The water glimmered in the moonlight and then came a *blub* sound and a ripple as a fish or a turtle surfaced and disappeared. Albert looked up at the purplish dark blue of the night sky and wished he had the power to make everything right.

# 6.1

*What do you think? Does he look like one of your kind?* Mehk asked Laika.

Tackle, standing in his new disguise, groaned. What dog in the history of dogs ever wore a disguise? Costumes, perhaps, for Halloween, which he'd never liked. But a disguise? *Grrrr.*

Laika looked at Tackle's new bearlike face and the twice-as-long tail. *Perfect. You're an artist, Mehk. I'm looking at a zawg here, not a dog! Amazing what you've done with so few resources.*

Mehk beamed.

*This smartskin itches,* Tackle said, shaking his head.

*I'm wearing a mask and I'm not complaining,* Mehk said.

Tackle stared at him. The botmaker was wearing the same disguise he had used to break out of prison—the mask and uniform of a Tev tech repairman. But he had changed the facial markings of the mask and had added a fake logo for a fake exterminator company to the jacket. The dog knew it was just a disguise, but Mehk's now-sneering Tev face with those distinctive tiger-like markings was giving him the heebie-jeebies.

After expressing thanks to Laika, they returned to their ITV and set off for Zeeno. Both were nervous, and their only conversation was to go over the plan. And then it was time to land.

*This will be our first challenge,* Mehk said as they approached Zeeno's capital. *I know they're tracking this vehicle and if Lat finds us—*

Just then, the ITV's alarm sounded and an audio message came through.

"This is Z-Tev Police. Hover and identify. Video on."

Quickly, Tackle curled up on the floor at Mehk's feet, pretending to sleep.

Mehk put the ITV in hover mode and the video snapped on. Two Z-Tev police officers, looking alarmed, leaned toward their camera lens. "Z-Tev citizen Si Cato here," Mehk said with a typical Z-Tev growl. "I am a pest exterminator reporting to prison number forty-seven."

"Run the vehicle code," one officer said to the other.

Tackle's muscles tensed, although he tried not to show it. Mehk had said that he had altered the digital code of the stolen ITV, but if what he did wasn't good enough, they could be discovered. Lat was surely waiting to pounce the moment that vehicle was found. They'd be dragged in for DNA scanning—or else just killed on the spot.

"I specialize in gheet removal," Mehk told the officers in a loud voice as the exterior port of the ITV was scanned and the code was retrieved and checked. "But I do everything. Gheets. Yits. Blucks. Soogers. You've got pests. I'll kill 'em. I'm the best." He sounded calm, but his foot, which was right by Tackle's head, was tapping the floor rapidly. *Tap. Tap. Tap. Tap. Tap. Tap. Tap.*

The Z-Tev's system beeped, and one officer told the other, "All clear."

Tackle opened one eye. Mehk's foot stopped.

"See you later!" Mehk said. "Don't forget! When the pests come out to play, I can make them go away!"

The video flicked off.

Mehk pushed the thruster forward and they zoomed toward Zeeno's capital.

As soon as they both knew they were out of sight, they stood up.

*Ha!* Mehk cheered. *I was brilliant!*

*Bravo!* Tackle wagged his long tail. Then he sat and looked up at Mehk. *Hey, now that we're out of danger, we should be able to send a message to Albert. We need to let him know the plan. He and the team could help.*

Mehk glanced at the dog. *You may be right.*

Tackle nodded. *I am right. Let me do the talking.*

# 6.2

In the park, as Albert stood at the dock's edge and stared at the cold pond's black water, his phone vibrated. He pulled out his phone and saw that it was an alien text.

Heart pounding, he read it.

*Tackle here, telling Mehk what to text. Mehk has finally had a change of heart! He is on our side. Believe me. He has a plan and it's a good one! We've been silent to stay safe. Now we're in disguise. We're on Zeeno. We're going to bust Zeenods out of prison, Albert! Lots of them. Our plan is to do it during the Gaböq game when all the Z-Tevs and Tevs are busy. I miss you and Trey, but this is good. You can trust this message. May this carrot bring you joy.*

Albert laughed out loud. May this carrot bring you joy! Their secret code. Tackle was not only all right, but Mehk was on their side. They were planning a prison breakout. This was amazing!

He looked up at the sky and grinned. Hope was back. Standing alone in that park, he made a silent vow to train harder than ever. He had a job to do. From now until game day, he was going to make use of every opportunity to improve. Filled with the desire to practice, he decided to make a leap right then and there. He looked around. Nobody in sight. Before he could talk himself out of it, he took off his coat, shirt, and pants, and—three, two, one—he jumped into the water. A crystal-clear pool in the middle of the day was one thing; a dark pond at night had a whole other vibe. His body tensed with fear the second he submerged. But he let the fear come and go, and then he opened his eyes and rose to the surface, keeping his movements calm and gentle. It wasn't that he was no longer afraid, it was that he was learning how to stay calm despite being afraid. That was the big difference.

Feeling triumphant, Albert floated on his back. The chill of the night air blew across his face but didn't bother him. He wondered if the Zeenods would allow him to keep the implants and adaptations after the johka tournament was over. Could he be part Star Striker forever or would he have to give it all up? Lightning Lee came to mind, and Albert wondered if, after all those years, Lee still had Star Striker advantages.

And then a frantic voice from the dock jolted him. "Albert!"

Jessica was standing there in the moonlight, calling out to him in shock.

Quickly he stammered that he was fine as he swam toward the dock. Embarrassed, he climbed out in his boxers and threw on his clothes and coat.

"Albert…what the—? I thought you were dead."

"I'm okay," he said. "I was just…swimming. It's a training thing. People do this. They swim in the winter to get their bodies adjusted to colder temperatures. I heard it's a good thing—"

"It's not good. It's crazy!" Jessica exclaimed. "Aren't you freezing? You've got to get dry. My dad isn't home, but I'll call for a ride—"

"No, don't call. I'm not cold. See? My training must be working."

She started pulling him in the direction of his house, handing him her hat.

"Thanks. You don't need to walk me home or give me your hat. I'm fine, Jessica. Really. This is a super-warm coat and I'm—Wait. What are you doing here? Why aren't you at the party?"

She opened her mouth and then closed it. And then she winced. "Promise not to tell?"

"Absolutely."

"I got nervous. I've got a lot on my mind and it was like the party was adding too much pressure so I texted Gabby and said I had to go to a thing with my dad." She pulled her hat back on. "Stupid, right? Wait. What are you doing here? I thought you had some gymnastics thing to go to?"

Now it was Albert's turn to wince. "Yeah. I made that up. I had a lot on my mind, too, and then the party made it more overwhelming." His heart pounded faster. "By the way, I wanted to explain something about that whole thing with Min."

"Yeah, Min told me she thought she was inviting Freddy but she invited you by mistake. She kept wanting to tell you but didn't know how to without hurting your feelings."

"The same thing happened to me!" Albert said quickly. "I said yes to her text inviting me to the party without even reading it! I thought she was asking me if I was all right after falling in the river. I didn't realize it was a party invitation."

"Oh." Jessica's face lit up. "I—I thought you liked her."

"I don't!" Albert said. "I mean, I like her as a friend, but I don't like her, you know, like as a—" He was too embarrassed to finish the sentence. "Anyway, I felt terrible and I was afraid if I said anything, she would be hurt and you would be mad at me for hurting her."

Jessica laughed. "You guys both screwed up."

Now was Albert's chance to tell Jessica that he had wanted to ask her to the party. He tried to do it, wondered why it was so hard, and then he fell silent.

They walked, heading out of the park.

Jessica was the next to speak. "When I said I had a lot of stuff on my mind, you said you had stuff on your mind, too. Did you mean besides the mix-up with Min?"

He couldn't tell her about Tackle or his life as a Star Striker for Zeeno, so he said, "Family stuff. What about you?"

She nodded. "Yeah. Family stuff."

He looked over at her, remembering how much he had assumed about her family that was wrong.

She went on. "My plan was to just stay home while the party was going on and watch something funny on TV and eat a ton of chocolate gelato. But then—" She stopped.

"What?"

"I found out my dad had a big date lined up for tonight at Buzzy's Diner with some mystery woman. A date! I got totally freaked out. So I decided to secretly walk over there and—you know—just sort of walk by the window to see them." She rolled her eyes. "That's where I was going when I saw you." She stopped. "Are you sure you're not cold?"

"Sure."

She shrugged. "Anyway. A stupid idea to spy on my dad, right?"

Albert shook his head. "Sounds totally reasonable to me."

"Thank you! This whole thing is getting to me."

"You really don't know who the mystery woman is?"

"I think it's this cashier at Trader Joe's. She's always flirting with him. I think they had a date last month."

He turned around. "So, let's go to Buzzy's and find out."

Jessica smiled. "Really?"

Albert nodded and they took off toward downtown.

They walked and for a while the conversation kept turning back to the temperature and how astounding it was that Albert wasn't cold. He wished he could tell her everything that was going on in his life. He didn't want to hold back.

The topic turned again to parents. "Is it wrong of me to want my dad to not date?" she asked.

He shook his head. "I get it. If my mom ever brought a dude home, I think I'd be furious."

"Thank you. Thank you. Thank you."

"I'm lucky," he added. "My mom is a workaholic. She has a million meetings. I can't see her ever dating."

They headed out of the park and onto the sidewalk. Albert felt lighter. Issues that had been stressing him out were not as stressful anymore. Finally, this whole thing with Min and Freddy and Jessica was over. He had felt like such a loser for lying to avoid the party, but Jessica had done the same thing. That helped.

They turned the corner and Buzzy's Diner came into view across the street and just down the block.

"No offense to your dad, but Buzzy's isn't exactly Valentine's material," Albert said. "I mean, if I wanted to impress a date, I don't think I'd pick Buzzy's."

"Yeah, you'd probably take your date for a freezing-cold swim," she said with a straight face.

He laughed.

"No, you're right about Buzzy's," she said. "My dad is totally clueless."

"Maybe that's a good thing," Albert said. "Maybe whoever he's in love with will think he's cheap and dump him."

Jessica laughed. "Oh my God, please let that happen."

Albert stopped. "You can't just walk by. What if they're sitting in the window? They'll see you."

"You walk by," Jessica said. "If you see them, stop and—"

He pulled out his phone. "Let's video chat while I'm walking. It'll look like I'm just talking on the phone, but I'll turn on the camera so you'll be able to see what I see."

"Brilliant!" she said. "If my dad sees you, just wave like it's no big deal. I'll wait here."

After they connected and he was crossing the street, he found himself grinning. He knew Jessica was anxious, but he had to admit it was fun being her spy. The whole night, which he had thought would be so terrible, was turning out to be fun. Maybe they could make this a regular thing—secretly stalking Mr. Sam.

"Slow down," Jessica's voice came through the phone. "Look natural."

"Okay, as you can see we're approaching the first window," he said. "Table of four really old people. Passing doorway. Approaching second window."

A young couple were at the small table in the window, but just beyond it in a booth Mr. Sam was sitting with—

Albert stopped.

"Hold it up," Jessica's voice came through the phone. "I can't see!"

Albert walked past the window quickly.

"Albert! Go back! I didn't get a good look. Who was that?"

Shocked, Albert leaned against the wall on the other side of the diner.

"Albert, who's his date?"

Albert took a breath. "My mom."

# 6.3

*Challenge number two,* Mehk whispered. The prison stood in front of them, gray and grim. *I never thought I'd come back here voluntarily.*

*We can do this,* Tackle said. *I'm ready.*

Mehk hoisted his tool bag onto his shoulder and they walked up the path and to the front gate.

Passing through the outside gate and in through the front foyer doors was no problem. It was Blocck that Mehk was worried about. There were four security guards by the entrance to the main hallway, and that's where Blocck's office window looked out. Last time, Mehk had snuck out at night when Blocck was off duty, but now that he was pretending to be an exterminator, he couldn't avoid him.

Trying to look as natural as a dog in zawg disguise could be, Tackle trotted next to Mehk.

"I have an appointment," the botmaker said, and flashed his fake exterminator ID at the guards. Out of the corner of his eye, he saw Blocck step out of his office.

One of the guards looked at Tackle and shook his head. "No animals allowed."

Mehk laughed. "Ridiculous. This zawg is essential."

The guards looked at each other, confused.

"What's this about?" Blocck asked.

Quickly Mehk flashed his ID again. "Didn't your last exterminator use a zawg?"

Now Blocck looked confused, although he tried not to show it.

"No wonder you have gheets!" Mehk went on. "Zawgs can sniff out gheet eggs before they hatch. I never work without one. I even live with one! You'll be glad you hired me! Got pests? I'm the best!"

Blocck looked at Tackle, who put his head down and immediately began to sniff around.

"You'll save money and time, too!" Mehk said. "With me, you don't need to spray every cell. I'll walk this zawg down the halls. One sniff at the doorways and he can tell me if we need to spray in that cell or not. With one thousand cells here, that will save time. And that means a big savings is guaranteed." He leaned in and whispered. "Of course, you don't have to tell the central office that. You can say you had to pay full price to have me spray every cell and you can give me my pay and keep the difference."

The tiniest smile appeared on Blocck's face. "As long as you get rid of these gheets, you can bring in a haagoolt for all I care. Let them through. My office first!"

The heavy doors opened, and Mehk and Tackle walked through.

Mehk held up a spray canister of fluid—it was just cleaning fluid he got from Laika that smelled horrible, but it looked official. "This fluid is powerful and can damage the optical ports of PEERs, so it'd best if I can send any PEER to dock in the hallway during a spray."

Blocck believed the lie and handed over a remote-control device that would enable Mehk to control any individual PEER. He also gave Mehk a security badge to open any and all doors without triggering alarms.

Hiding their delight, Mehk and Tackle got to work—inspecting the offices first and setting off to do the cells. Every now and again Tackle did find gheets or gheet eggs—he was, after all, truly good at sniffing them out. But instead of killing them, Mehk secretly scooped them up and put them in the side pocket of his tool bag.

As they walked up the stairs toward the cells on the second

floor, Mehk whispered, *This will be Kayko's floor. Remember, sniff every doorway, but just bark at Kayko's cell. I'll tell you when we get there. It's the tenth cell from the stairs.*

He didn't tell Tackle that the reason he knew her location was because he had promised the Zeenods once before that he would free her.

Tackle stopped. *Wait. We have the device and the badge, why don't we just open all the doors and let the Zeenods out now? With a thousand rushing at the doors, the guards will be overpowered.*

Mehk shook his head. *We can't control every PEER at the same time with this controller. If the Zeenods walked out now, most of them would be killed by their own PEERs. It's the PEERs that are the biggest obstacle, not the guards. We still have to deal with them. Now shhh!*

When they passed through the stair doorway to the second-floor hallway, the PEERs outside every cell door blinked and whirred. Tackle began his job of sniffing at the crack under each door, trying to look at the hovering drones without being obvious. They were mean-looking metal machines with rotating wings, weaponized arms, and an awful moving eye in the belly that Tackle knew was a camera.

Finally, Mehk gave Tackle the signal that they had reached Kayko's cell. As agreed, Tackle sniffed at the crack under Kayko's cell door and then howled.

"Gheet eggs inside this cell? Good boy!" Mehk said loudly, and patted Tackle's head. Quickly, the botmaker used the remote-control device to activate the PEER's docking protocol so that it wouldn't follow them inside, and then he swiped his security badge over the door's optical port to open it.

Mehk walked in to see a thin and anxious Kayko sitting on her bed. He was struck by how much the athletic and healthy Zeenod had changed. Her green eyes looked exhausted, but curiosity flashed in them when what looked like a zawg trotted in next.

"We are here to exterminate gheets," Mehk said, and gave Tackle his second signal. To help cover up the conversation, Tackle was supposed to make as much noise as possible, so the dog barked, growled, and howled. For his part, Mehk used the trick he had learned when he had been stuck in the same prison: to sing. Because the PEERs were not programmed to record singing, the Zeenods sang whatever speech they wanted to keep a secret.

"*Kayko, I am a Zeenod,*" Mehk chanted softly.

Kayko stood, her bem lifting, but as soon as he sang his name, she stepped away from him and stiffened. "*Mehklen Pahck, your betrayal of the Zeenods here was beyond hurtful,*" she sang her anger back to him.

"*I know. All of the Zeenods here worked together to free you, Kayko. Instead I used the Zeenods to free myself. I can't deny that is a chapter in my story.*" Mehk shrugged. "*But not all of my story. I am not the same Mehk. I'm committed, now, to using my intelligence to return Zeeno to the Zeenods. I am working with Albert Kinney, and to prove it, I have his dog here in disguise.*"

Speechless, Kayko turned to stare at Tackle.

*It's true,* Tackle quickly whispered, knowing that Kayko could understand Dog. *Albert and the Zeenods miss you and have not lost hope.*

Kayko crouched down and looked deeply into Tackle's eyes. Her face began to soften, and then that familiar light returned to her eyes. She stood and Tackle resumed his noisemaking.

"*What are you here to do?*" Kayko sang.

"*It will take some time,*" Mehk continued, "*but I will be introducing a virus to the PEERs. This virus will change the coding of the PEERs and allow each Zeenod to gain control of each PEER through voice activation. Once this happens, the Zeenods can use their PEERs to escape. Not just from this prison, but from as many prisons as possible! We are planning an uprising to occur and want it to occur during a johka game, when the guards and wardens will be watching the game. We are hoping to be ready for this coming game. I will be back when I've succeeded and will give you more information then."*

A guard's footsteps could be heard walking down the hallway, and Mehk acted the role of exterminator, yelling at Kayko to sit on her hygg and then spraying the cleaning fluid in each corner of the cell.

*"Tell the other Zeenods,"* Mehk sang softly as they prepared to leave. *"Everyone must work together to achieve success."*

Kayko's face softened. *"Mehk, this is what Zeenods do best."* And then her bem shifted slightly and she added, *"I'm glad you have returned."*

Mehk beamed. He was surprised by how good it felt to connect with Kayko. *"When I developed my original plan of getting Albert to quit, I underestimated all of you. I underestimated you, Albert, Tackle, and all the Zeenods. The Zeenods here in the prison, too,"* he confessed. *"Determination, passion, and intelligence—these are traits I admire and traits that are in all of you."* Mehk bowed.

Kayko returned the bow, her eyes turning gold.

*"I look forward to seeing old Zin walk free,"* Mehk sang. *"He knew my parents and is my ahnparent, as you probably know."*

Tears brimmed and Kayko put a hand to her heart. *"Zin died last week."*

Mehk was speechless for a moment, lost in regret. He thought of the old Zeenod's kind face and how trusting he had been.

Tackle sensed movement in the hallway and nudged Mehk.

Kayko put a hand on his shoulder. *"May whatever arises serve to remind you of the power of the ahn,"* she sang.

Mehk nodded.

As they left, Tackle turned and got one more look at Albert's beloved coach before the cell door slammed shut.

*Now that the message is delivered, let's get out of here,* Tackle whispered.

*We need to pretend to inspect the whole prison,* Mehk said. *Plus I need to steal one thing before we go.*

Anxious to get out, Tackle moved down the hallway quickly. *Sniff. Trot. Sniff. Trot.*

They sprayed a few more cells, so it wouldn't look suspicious that they only found eggs in Kayko's. In the stairway, Mehk took the risk of uploading the coding system for the PEER protocols from the remote-control device to his own portable computer. Then came the last task. Mehk stopped in front of the office of PEER repairs and gave Tackle the signal. Tackle sniffed and then howled.

At that, Mehk barged in and ordered the service technician to clear the room so he could spray it. Happy to take a break, the Z-Tev left. As soon as he was gone, Mehk walked over to a shelf crowded with deactivated PEERs and slipped one into the bottom of his exterminator bag. He needed a PEER to develop and test his code. Quickly he covered it with a cloth, placed the sprayer and fluid cans on top, and zipped it up.

*Now we can go,* Mehk whispered.

Relieved to be done, Tackle almost enjoyed the long walk back to the front hallway. Without incident they walked past the warden's window. At the final exit, Mehk had to hand over the badge and the remote controller to two Z-Tevs guarding the exit. That was no problem. But then they said they had to inspect his bag. Tackle's heart pounded, but the guards barely looked inside before zipping it back up and waving them on.

And then, just as they were opening the door, they heard Blocck's voice.

"Stop!"

They both froze and then slowly turned.

Blocck walked forward and handed Mehk an electronic chip. "Your payment."

"Ah!" Mehk took it. "Of course. Thank you."

"I have to tell you I have my doubts about you exterminators. The last one I hired clearly didn't do his job."

"Trust me," Mehk said. "My work here will truly surprise you! Oh, and we'll be back to do a free inspection."

"If I find a single gheet, I'll demand the whole payment back and charge you for wasting my time," grumbled Blocck, and he turned back toward his office. "I hate those gheets."

Smiling, Mehk and Tackle walked out the door.

# 7.0

The next month was a blur for Albert. The discovery of the secret date between Albert's mom and Jessica's dad at Buzzy's Diner had a strange effect on his budding friendship with Jessica. She just stopped talking to him. And it had an even stranger effect on his relationship with his mom and Erin and Nana. He couldn't stop thinking about it, but he didn't want to think about it, so he just kept shoving the whole subject down, which meant avoiding everyone as much as possible. It was all so awkward and exactly what he didn't need.

He was missing Tackle terribly, although he was proud of his canine friend for everything he was doing. If he'd been able to hang out with Tackle, he wouldn't have been so on edge. Tackle always had a way of calming him down. And the more he missed Tackle, the more he wanted to avoid Trey, who was worried sick for good reason.

All Albert could do was focus on training, which he did, determined to improve physically and mentally. The weeks passed, and then game weekend finally arrived.

Before the last game against Jhaateez, Albert had missed the ritual sleepover because Lat had kidnapped him and sent him hurtling to Gravespace GJ7. For this trip, he was understandably nervous. But, thankfully, the trip was uneventful and he arrived on Gaböq in time to catch the other game in the tournament—Tev against Jhaateez.

The team watched it together on a big screen in their bleak Gaböq hotel. Early in the game, Linnd was injured, and that rattled the confidence of the Jhaateezians. Soon after, Vatria scored two goals—and Albert hated to admit it, but they were beautiful. Finally the Jhaateezians got one back, but then a massive Tev midfielder broke out and scored a third for Tev, and then Vatria scored one more. A huge win for the Tevs: 4–1. Vatria was actually smiling at the medal ceremony.

Albert and the Zeenods were crushed. This meant that if they progressed to the final game, they'd have to face off against Vatria and the Tevs. He tried to shake off the dread and focus on the game at hand.

Before Albert knew it, morning arrived, and he was walking onto the Gaböq field with his team. The stadium was bleak and quiet. The atmosphere was all business. No pregame music. No vendors. The stands were full, but tensely somber. This was the Gaböq team's last chance to win at least a little honor and a little reward.

Carved into the stadium's rock walls were enormous portraits of famous Gaböqs with their three crocodile-like eyes staring down at the field. The effect made Albert feel tiny and surrounded.

A trumpet sounded and out strode Xutu and the Gaböq players. They were so huge—awkward and yet graceful. After they lined up on the field, each player stood like a statue, wide mouth clamped shut, all three eyes staring straight ahead.

After the official medical scans were done, the Gaböq anthem was played, and Albert hardly noticed. He was running through a checklist in his mind of all the possible ways to avoid the fissures. But then the Zeenod anthem began and Albert looked up to see brave Zeenods who had traveled from other planets to support them. They were standing and singing with pride. The planetary crests were exchanged next. And when the images of Zeeno's most beautiful features—the vacha trees, the ahda birds, the zees—were projected on huge screens for the crowd to see, Albert's heart leaped. Zeeno was once so beautiful! He was here because everything beautiful was in danger of being wiped out. All because of Tev's ruthless aggression. Deep in his chest, he felt that buzzing of ahn energy building. He looked around at his teammates. They were all standing, tall and proud, their eyes shining. They had worked hard and risked their lives to play in this tournament. And somewhere out there Tackle and Mehk were working hard on behalf of Zeeno, right now. He didn't know where they were or what exactly they were doing, but he knew they were out there.

Albert closed his eyes, sending his ahn energy out toward the Zeenods on the field and the Zeenods in the stands. Let's do this, he thought.

And then the two Star Strikers were asked to step forward.

Albert and Xutu bowed and repeated the Fŭigor Johka Federation vow in unison. "As a representative of my planet, I promise to play to the best of my ability, to respect you as my competitor, and to uphold the rules of the game."

Xutu sneered and lifted his foot. Engraved in the Gabŏq dirt: **AK=FAILURE**.

Albert noticed the quickening of his heartbeat, but he took a breath and added the silent meditation: *May we both play well.*

After Gabŏq won the coin toss and places were announced, Albert walked to the center of the field. The Gabŏqs' massive footprints were everywhere. **ZEENO=WEAKNESS. ZEENO=SHAME**.

Doz, Albert noticed, was trying to scuff them out as he walked to his spot on the field. "We are strong. We are proud. We are Zeenods!" Doz yelled.

Albert and his teammates chanted back. "We are strong. We are proud. We are Zeenods!"

# 7.1

*The game is about to start,* Tackle called out to Mehk. *Look, there's Albert!*

The dog was sitting in front of a laptop that was on the floor, his caramel-colored eyes glued to the sight of Albert on the small screen. *Gabŏq has the first kick. Go, Albert! Go, Zeenods!*

Mehk was sitting at a small table. On it, the PEER he had stolen was humming quietly but not moving. For the thirteenth time, Mehk leaned in and said loudly, "Hover!" The machine's blades didn't budge.

With the money that Mehk had received as exterminator, he and Tackle had been able to pay for a hotel in Zeeno's capital. There, among the other guests, the two worked, keeping up their disguises whenever they had to go out. Mostly, they stayed inside. Mehk had been working on the code to reprogram the PEERs to follow the voice commands of the Zeenods, but each time he had tried to test it on the PEER, something had gone wrong. And the money was running out.

"Hover!" he shouted.

*I don't think yelling is going to make a difference,* Tackle said, not taking his eyes off the screen.

Mehk struck himself on the side of the head. *I wanted to be ready by today. Time is slipping by too fast.* He hit himself again and again.

*Hey…Hey…Stop that, Mehk.* Tackle got up and gently put a paw on the botmaker's arm. *If you're not ready, you're not ready. Hitting yourself doesn't help. Take a break and watch the game. When it's over, let's go out and play a game ourselves. Run around a little. Chase a ball. That'll get the juices flowing. Then we can get back to work. Sound good?* Tackle waited, his head cocked to the side, his eyes full of compassion.

The last weeks hadn't been easy on either of them. They were constantly tired, constantly on alert, and barely had enough to eat.

Mehk looked at the dog, at his expressive face, his black nose, his velvety ears, and his glossy reddish coat. A rush of gratitude hit. He had thought his animatronic gheet was the best possible companion, but this Earth dog? Well, this dog was next-level.

He took a breath and turned to watch the game.

# 7.2

The ball floated into place, the trumpet blared, and it was game on. Xutu started and passed the ball back to their center mid. A shaky pass. The Gaböq's center mid tried to pass to their outside back, but this one was sloppy, too. Albert sensed right away that Xutu and the Gaböqs were hypertense. He recalled a lesson from Ennjy about the difference between playing to beat and playing your best. Playing to beat means you focus on controlling your opponent's performance, which makes you feel tense. Playing your best means you focus on controlling your own performance, which makes you feel powerful.

The Gaböqs were playing to beat, Albert thought. And Albert's teammates noticed the Gaböqs' tense energy, too. Instinctively the Zeenods pulled in tight to defend, the ahn energy between them strengthening. Stay steady, Albert told himself. No need to press.

Patient and alert, Albert and the Zeenods let the Gaböqs keep passing with their heavy first touches.

It was odd to see such huge beasts galloping with that strange tripedal gait. They were able to swivel and pivot in surprising ways with their huge yet oddly springy limbs. For the first few minutes, Albert just tried to get used to being near them on the field. They grunted frequently and smelled like meat that had been out in the sun too long.

And then an opening occurred. Uncomfortable in possession and desperate to score, the Gaböq center mid prepared to send a direct ball back up top to Xutu. But Doz, in a perfect position to defend, lit up. As soon as the touch hit Xutu's blocky right hammer, Doz pounced. Now the Zeenods had the ball.

Luckily the Gaböq sun stayed behind the clouds. No fissures. No problem. The Zeenods pulled off a series of tight passes, and their tiki-taka style was a perfect counterpoint. Quickly, Albert and the Zeenods had the Gaböqs on edge. Soon Doz had the ball again and he passed to Heek, who made a nice move on a Gaböq defender to play a give-and-go with Giac. Next it went to Heek, who was down the line. Albert ran to the top of the box. In dangerous territory, Heek glanced up and saw Albert making his run.

Albert didn't even have to call for it. Heek played it. A solid pass.

Big breath. Albert met the ball, and the next thing he knew, that ball went zinging into the back of the net.

Albert turned to look at his teammates, and then a jubilant laugh burst out.

"Yes!" Ennjy shouted. "That's Zeenod teamwork!"

And then, just as cheers from the Zeenods and fans in the audience were rising, the deep voice of the Gaböq announcer boomed across the stadium. Albert expected to hear "Goal for Zeeno" but instead the announcer shouted, "Shame to Gaböq!" His voice boomed as if it were coming from a god in the sky. "One to zero. Failure for Gabóq." The eerie sound of hissing followed from the Gabóqs and their allies in the stadium.

Albert froze, hardly believing his ears. And then Doz shrugged. "Here, they focus on who lost the goal, not who won it."

"I'm happy I don't live here," Albert said.

For the next twenty minutes, the Zeenods played hard and communicated well. The sun stayed behind the clouds, and Albert almost felt like he was playing soccer back on Earth. Already he was getting used to the sights and smells on the field. More often than not, he and his teammates kept possession, and they had two more goal-scoring opportunities—both stopped by the Gabóq keeper, who was way more agile than Albert expected.

At the twenty-second minute, the Gabóqs got the ball and sent it long and hard to their left winger. Wayt was ready and outraced him. And then, just as Wayt pulled the ball around to pass it, the sun blazed through and a fissure began to open up in front of him. He pivoted to avoid it, not realizing that a rare second fissure had opened. Assuming he would not have to deal with two at once, Wayt was caught off guard. He froze, isolated on a strip of ground just to the left of the box.

In that split second, Xutu ran and jumped into the biggest part of the first fissure and plunged down, pulling all the Zeenods' attention with him. At the same time, another Gabóq player hopped over the second fissure and stole the ball from Wayt. It all happened in an instant. Wayt woke up and tried to wrestle the ball away, but by this time, Xutu was shooting back up through the first fissure. The winger played a cross that sailed up and over the fissure just as Xutu came shooting back up. With dread, Albert just knew what was going to happen next. Xutu's massive head connected with the ball, and the ball found the top corner of the net.

Goal!

"Shame to Zeeno!" the announcer bellowed.

Now the Gabōqs and their allies went wild, stamping and cheering, standing on their rear legs and raising their huge front legs up to the sky. Within seconds, thick clouds crowded out the light and the fissures closed.

"One to one!" the announcer said, and there were more cheers.

Albert looked around. His teammates were as shaken as he was.

"Keep the focus," Ennjy called out as the game resumed.

But very quickly another fissure opened up, and the Gabōqs used it to get another goal.

Two to one. Gabōq.

"We have the ahn!" Ennjy called out. "We need to use it!"

Amped up by their lead, the Gabōq players were on fire, and it took every ounce of Zeenod energy to defend. Toben saved another goal. And then, just the before the end of the first half, the Zeenods pulled in and got possession again. The rhythm was right, and they quickly moved the ball up. Ennjy set up a perfect pass to Sormie, who was in a great position at the top of the box. Albert was running to follow up when the clouds shifted and the ground beneath Sormie's feet began to move.

"Watch out!" Albert shouted.

Sormie tripped on a bulge just as a fissure opened. *BAM!* Flat on her face. Under her torso, the ground began to pull apart. Stretched out over the widening crack, she held on to one side as the ball floated next to her.

Albert ran. But instead of going for the ball, he stopped and crouched to help Sormie up.

*Boom!*—a Gabōq defender jumped across the fissure, kicking the ball long to Xutu.

Albert and Sormie stood up just as Xutu sliced the ball in for another goal.

"Shame to Zeeno!" the announcer's gleeful voice echoed in the huge stadium. "Three to one. Zeeno down."

And it was halftime.

# 7.3

As soon as the Zeenods hit the locker room, Sormie turned to Albert and shouted. "I didn't need help! You should have gone for the ball!"

"But you looked like you were going to fall! I—"

"You assumed wrong, Albert! You cost us that goal."

Wayt stepped in. "I made a mistake, too. Because I assumed we wouldn't see two fissures at once, I was caught by surprise."

"All our shawbles are coming out!" Sormie nearly sobbed.

Ennjy held up a hand. "Listen. Our opponents are playing well. We have a choice right now. We can get tied up in regret. Or we can learn from what happened and go out and play stronger."

Sormie straightened up and wiped her tears. "Sorry, Albert."

Albert turned to her. "I shouldn't have assumed you needed me."

Ennjy put one hand on Albert's shoulder and one hand on Sormie's shoulder. "We have all trained. We need to trust in the training. And we need to stay focused and calm. Remember, the

Gaböqs don't just want to win. They want us to become desperate enough to break a rule—to cheat or to attack a ref—so that we will be disqualified from the tournament. They're going to push us in the second half. We need to be prepared."

Doz nodded. "The fissures are messing with our minds. But Ennjy is right. Let's stay focused and calm! What are fissures? Little cracks. So what if we fall through? We can deal with it. We can do this! We have each other. We have the ahn." Doz looked at Albert and grinned, his huge eyes full of affection. "Full steam in the head!"

Albert stood tall and pounded the air with his fist. "Full steam in the head!"

# 7.4

After halftime, the Gaböqs came out throwing insults, trying to tempt the Zeenods into fighting, but Albert and his teammates stayed strong and ignored them. The ahn was flowing again, and the Zeenods possessed to draw out the Gaböq defense. Ten minutes in, they found a hole to play Ennjy through. Now it was just the keeper to beat.

Calmly, Ennjy sent one of her beautiful strikes—one that curved at the end. The keeper dove too far to the left, and the ball just nicked his right shoulder as it went in.

"Goal!" Albert shouted. "Goal!" Over the obnoxious shaming of the Gaböqs, Albert lifted his arms up to the Zeenods in the stadium, encouraging them to chant with him. "Goal! Goal!"

"It's three to two," Ennjy said. "Let's tie it up."

In the next ten minutes, two more fissures opened—neither near Albert. Both times, his Zeenod teammates were ready. Giac used her bem to prevent her from falling into one. And Feeb deftly jumped across the other one. All the while they continued using their tight passes to keep possession.

Albert knew his focus was split between the game and the ground, and he tried hard to let go of his fear. And then, a determined Sormie, who felt so terrible about her earlier mistake, managed to dodge two attackers and score another goal.

Three to three. A tie with ten minutes left! What a game.

The Gaböqs were furious. Taking a chance, one of their defenders sent a long ball to their center midfielder, who walloped it on to Xutu. Beeda slid in to win the ball, and two Gaböqs immediately attacked her. After she managed to pass it to Doz, one of the Gaböqs knocked her to the ground with deliberate force.

Albert's gaze shot to Reeda, hoping she wouldn't lose her cool. But the ref stopped the game and called a foul.

"An accident!" The Gaböq offered a ridiculous excuse, but the ref saw through it and did the right thing. He removed the player from the game.

When Reeda went to help Beeda up, another Gaböq grinned and grunted, "You're next."

She lunged to strike him, but Doz rushed in to hold her back. "They planned this! They're trying to get us to react!"

Wincing in pain, Beeda stood tall. "They cannot get to us."

A rush of pride ran through Albert. "Let's win this!"

Play resumed and within a few minutes the chance for a goal came. Reeda sent a deep ball flying over the midfield line. Just gorgeous. Albert ran toward it, wide open. He knew the other forwards were positioning themselves. But then Albert felt a shifting of light and he looked up to see the clouds part. No, he thought. No, no, no, no! In the next second, his footing was nonexistent. Down he plunged.

# 7.5

The second Albert hit the water, his ability to reason dissolved. One thought screamed an endless loop in his brain: Real eels. Real eels. Real eels. Real eels.

He kicked his way back up to the surface, and as his lungs filled with air, his inner voice came through. Calm down, Albert. The grythers are going to come, but you do not have to react to them. Heart pounding, he shifted onto his back and told his arms and legs to relax.

Above him, he watched the fissure close, and the terror of being alone started to churn inside his chest. Hold on, he told himself, the fissures open and the fissures close. That's what they do. You don't need to react to them.

To remain calm, he focused on the gold light from his uniform that was bouncing off the ceiling. He could feel the gentle current of the river and knew he was floating toward the exit. He was doing well. All he had to do was pretend he was floating in the practice facility or in his pool back home.

Out of the corner of his eye, he saw the first gryther and then another and another. Instinct kicked in, and he started backstroking sloppily. But immediately, he could feel the vibrations of energy in the water change. Float, Albert. Float. He closed his eyes and resumed floating. An eel head brushed against his shoulder.

I will not react.

Another eel slithered up and over his belly for one, two, three, four, five, six, seven seconds before it was gone.

He was doing it. He was staying calm. A tiny smile lit his face. Again, he focused on the ceiling and the way the light was dancing on it. He wanted to shift his position so he could look out and see how far he was from the exit, but instead, he told himself to hold his position. The exit would come when it would come. His looking at it wouldn't make it come any faster.

The under-river he was floating in joined another, and for a few minutes he drifted into the center of a larger body of water. The thought that he was farther away now from any sides or ledges sent a new rush of anxiety through him. But he let the thought come and go and he kept floating.

A minute later, he passed the carved mark in the ceiling that came right before the exit. And then he saw the hatch. Gently he steered his body to float toward the side and then slowly swam the last bit toward the ladder, careful not to splash. Finally, he climbed out of the river. When he was standing on solid ground, he allowed himself a moment of joy.

"Yes!" he shouted, and his voice echoed off the cavern walls. "Yes! Yes! Yes!" He started dancing. "I did it! I did it!"

Eager to join his team, he climbed up the ladder, and when he got to the highest rung, he reached for the hatch handle. It wouldn't turn.

He pushed and pounded against the thick metal door, trying again and again and calling out for help. For a full minute, he kept pounding, until his hand was bruised and sore. This was no accident. Someone had locked that door.

He climbed down, picked up the nearest rock he could find, and threw it up at the hatch. It struck against the metal and tumbled down, bouncing from the ledge back into the water. Instantly a trio of eels approached to check out the commotion. The sight of them made Albert want to throw up.

Suddenly a rumbling sound came from a distance ahead. He watched a crack appear in the ceiling upstream—past center field, he guessed—and then a Gaböq plunged down. For a brief moment, the sounds of the roaring crowd could be heard through the crack.

"Hey!" Albert shouted.

Then, like a torpedo, the player shot back out of the water.

"Hey!" Albert shouted again. But the Gaböq sailed through the crack and the fissure closed.

Albert stood in the silence that followed. All he could hear was the sound of the water slapping against the ledges. Grythers slithered toward the disturbance, not knowing that the Gaböq who had plunged down was already gone.

What was he supposed to do now, Albert wondered? Clearly, the Gaböqs wanted him down here for the rest of the game. And then a thought occurred to him. What if the Gaböqs were working with the Tevs? What if the Gaböqs had deliberately locked the exit to harm them?

He had to find a way out.

Cautiously he walked along the thin ledge, determined to move upstream and find another exit. He was beginning to give up hope when another rumbling came quite nearby. Albert looked up and saw a fissure opening above the river, only about five feet ahead of him. Xutu plunged down, his back toward Albert. Without even thinking, Albert knew what he was going to do. Heading straight for the same spot in the water where Xutu had plunged in, Albert jumped. He slammed against Xutu just as Xutu shot back up. With a piggybacked hug, Albert wrapped his arms and legs around the striker's muscular back leg and held on tight. Up they rose, and by the time Xutu realized why he felt heavier than usual, they were through the fissure and the sounds and sights and smells of the johka stadium were back.

As Xutu reached the top of his trajectory, he grunted and gave a mighty twist, the force of which sent Albert flying. Okay, now I'm going to die, Albert thought as he sailed through the air, but then he landed against a Zhidorian referee, whose squidlike body softened the blow.

At the same time, Xutu connected with the ball and sliced it into the goal.

Four to three, Gaböq.

The crowd went crazy.

# 7.6

Albert untangled himself from the Zhidorian's tentacles. "They locked the emergency exit!" he shouted as loudly as he could.

The wide gash of Xutu's mouth wanted to smile. Albert was sure he saw it begin before Xutu regained control.

"Impossible!" the Gaböq tactician yelled.

"I'm telling the truth!" Albert shouted back.

A team of FJF officials gathered and went with the Gaböq tactician to inspect the hatch. They descended and returned with their verdict.

"No malfunction. Player error."

Albert and the team were about to go ballistic and the Gaböqs were encouraging them to go for it when Ennjy ordered her team to calm down. With her extraordinary presence, she stood tall and looked at her teammates. Her bem was pulsing. Her violet eyes were shining. Although she didn't say a word, Albert and the others could understand what she was communicating to them. If the Gaböqs had gone so far as to sabotage the exit, they would have planned to make sure the hatch was working upon inspection. Now, they were hoping the Zeenods would start a fight.

Albert looked at this teammates. They were responding to Ennjy's silent message by standing tall, breathing in and out, and connecting through the ahn. So smart. A rush of pride went through him. The way for the Zeenods to win this game was not by attacking the Gaböqs. All they had to do was play their best and do nothing to disqualify them from advancing to the final match.

With quiet strength, Ennjy turned and bowed to the officials. "Although we disagree, we accept your decision."

The Gaböqs sneered.

Unfazed, the Zeenod team took their places to make the final push, but seconds after the play started, the final trumpet blared.

The game was over. Four to three, Gaböq.

Although a part of Albert wanted to scream and protest, he followed Ennjy's lead. With dignity, they all stood in place as the Gaböq celebration went forward. The Gaböqs had lost their last chance to stay in the tournament, but they had won the match—even if it was through cheating—and they were determined to celebrate. Gaböq singers came out and faced the Zeenods. On cue they stood on their rear legs and sang a horrible song in Gaböq that basically repeated the line *"Shame to Zeeno"* over and over while glowing animatronic eels slithered around on the field. Albert wanted to throw his cleats at them.

To hand out the medals to the Gaböq team, the Gaböq president walked past each of the Zeenods, dangling the medals first in front of the Zeenods as the crowd hissed.

"They're the ones who should be ashamed," Albert muttered.

Next to him, Doz nodded. "But you are alive, Albert. I thought the grythers got you. We can celebrate that after this is over."

Albert could have hugged him on the spot.

There were closing remarks, and then the FJF officials announced what everyone already knew: the results of the tournament so far.

"In round one, Zeeno and Jhaateez won their games against Tev and Gaböq. In round two, Tev and Zeeno won their games against Gaböq and Jhaateez. In round three, Tev and Gaböq won their games against Jhaateez and Zeeno."

On huge screens, the scores flashed.

"Gaböq and Jhaateez each have one win. Zeeno and Tev are tied for two wins. Zeeno and Tev will play in the final round."

The loudest cheers in the stadium came from the Tevs and their allies.

The FJF did a four-sided die toss to determine the location of the final game. In Fŭigor tradition, all four of the planets that were participating in the tournament were possible hosts, and those planet names had been engraved on the four sides of the die.

Please let it be Zeeno, Albert chanted to himself. Please let it be Zeeno.

The die was thrown. "It's Tev!" the official called out, and the Tevs in the audience stood and cheered again.

# 8.0

When Albert woke up, the first thing he noticed was the quiet and his first thought was panic. Many people would think a quiet house suggests peace. To Albert, it suggested the possibility that his entire family had been kidnapped by aliens.

Quickly, he hopped out of bed and picked up his phone. A text from his mom explained that she had taken Erin to gymnastics. *Whew.* And Nana explained her absence in a long voice mail. She had gone to New York for a series of last-minute meetings regarding some nature-education grants she had been working on for her school and she wasn't sure when she'd be done. Albert took another breath, relieved she was okay but missing her already. He had gotten used to having Nana around. She had a way of calming him down, of knowing what he needed, and he needed her now more than ever! Again, he listened to the end of her message.

*Albert, I'm sorry I have to skedaddle for a bit. Just wanted to say that I've loved spending so much time with you this past year and have been so proud to see how much stronger you've grown. Yes, physically. But even more importantly, you've grown as a person. That old broken hip of mine, which kept me from flying home for so long, ended up being something that brought us closer. See, you never know what life will bring. Even the cloud of a broken bone can have a silver lining. May whatever clouds drift your way help you to be even stronger and wiser than you already are. I can tell there is a lot on your mind right now. We are overdue for a heart-to-heart. You've been isolating yourself. Spending time alone in your room can sometimes make you feel peaceful, but other times it just makes you feel alone. Take a walk in the park. Talk to the trees and birds. They're among the best listeners and teachers on this old planet of ours. Even if you feel alone, you're not alone. Love, Nana.*

Albert set down his phone and looked out his bedroom window. He tried to imagine what Nana would say if she knew what was really on his mind. If she knew that he'd almost been killed on a planet called Gaböq and that he was scheduled to play on another planet called Tev, if he could get there without being kidnapped or murdered and—

He stopped and focused on what his eyes could see outside the window instead of what was rumbling around in his mind. The sun was shining. The trees were budding. It was March 21. Somehow winter was over and spring had come and Nana knew he would feel better if he "talked" to the trees and birds. He downed some orange juice, stuffed a bagel and an apple in his coat pocket, put on his in-line skates for fun, and headed out.

His heart wrenched when there was no Tackle to greet him, but he took off. He hadn't been skating in months, and it felt great. When he arrived at the entrance to the park, he stopped and looked out at the green expanse. "Hello, world," he said.

The trees were beautiful, their new leaves unfurling silently. And the birds! Without even seeing them, he heard their presence. One calling. Another answering. And then from somewhere else, a different chorus of chirps and trills and melodies. His experience with Tackle had convinced him that all animals communicated with an intelligence that most humans couldn't appreciate. And he knew from Toben and Ennjy that trees could communicate, too, with each other and with other living things. They were all connected. The trees were relying on the birds to spread their seeds and control leaf-eating insects. The birds were relying on the trees to give them oxygen, food, and shelter. They were all on the same team, and Albert was a part of that team, too.

He pulled his Z-da from its hiding place under his shirt and rubbed his fingertips over the miniature scene of Zeeno that was embedded on the back: those blossoming vacha trees, the flock of multicolored ahda birds in the air, and the zees shooting up from the center of a valley. All these had once flourished on Zeeno, and he ached at the thought of their extinction at the hands of Tevs and Z-Tevs. By tearing down the trees to build more and more, the Z-Tevs were not just killing individual trees, but were also cutting off the chance for everything to communicate and connect, which was essential for survival.

Albert took in a deep breath of oxygen and released his carbon dioxide into the air. Yes, they had lost on Gaböq. Yes, they had a difficult job ahead of them. For sure, clouds were coming his way. Not just clouds. Freaking gigantic storms. But he was alive and he had to fight for what was right with his team.

Feeling stronger and wiser, he turned onto the park path, and when the skate park came into view, so did Jessica. The sight of her carving around the bowl of the skate park on her board made him realize how much he had missed hanging out with her this past month. Two things had taken the wheels out of their friendship: his training, and finding out that secret about their parents. They had to get their friendship back on track.

"Hey," he said.

She hopped onto the deck and watched him skate toward her. "Hey, Albert. You haven't been skating in a while. I figured you gave it up."

"I've been doing this other training," he said, keeping it vague.

"Yeah," she said. "Don't tell me you're jumping into ponds again?"

He smiled. "That's over." He dropped in, and she followed on her board.

They crisscrossed around the bowl for a while, and then he asked her if she was hungry. "I brought an apple and a bagel." He had thought he might feel nervous around her, but all that talking to the trees and birds had calmed him down.

They moved to a bench and he tore the bagel in half and handed a piece to her. "How are you?" he asked. "I mean about the whole parent thing."

"I'm still freaking out," she said.

"Did you talk to your dad about it?"

"No. Did you talk to your mom about it?"

He shook his head. "No." He pulled out his apple and she took a bite and handed it back.

"Where is your mom right now?" she asked.

"She took Erin to gymnastics."

"Are you sure?"

"Why?"

"My dad said he had another 'school meeting' to go to," she said. "He went back to Buzzy's, though. I secretly followed him and saw him go in, but then I chickened out and came here."

"Oh my God," Albert said. "My mom could be there. She always drops Erin off at the gym and says she's running errands. How many errands can you run?"

"It would be terrible if our parents, like, got together for real, right? I mean, it's not just me freaking out about this, right? What if they got married? What if we had to suddenly live together?"

Albert imagined Jessica walking around the house in her pajamas, Jessica finding his underwear in the dryer, Jessica barging in on him in the bathroom. He realized that the anxiety about their parents dating had been adding to his overall worries more than he had thought. He handed her the apple and pulled out his phone.

"What are you doing?"

"Getting an answer," he said, and read his message aloud as he texted.

*Mom, are you dating Mr. Sam?*

"Oh my God. Albert!" Jessica leaned in.

They waited. No reply.

Albert stood up. "Let's go. Let's walk right into Buzzy's and make them face us."

"You have skates on."

"I'll skate in and make them face us."

She stood up. "Okay. Let's do it."

Five minutes later they were staring, speechless, through the window at their parents sitting in a booth together.

"This is really happening," she said.

"Jessica? Albert?" A voice made them jump.

It was Gabby Fiero's mom.

"Um, hi," Jessica said.

"I'm late again!" the woman said, flustered. "I've been late to every meeting."

Albert glanced at Jessica.

"Meeting?" Jessica asked.

A phone began to ring, and Gabby's mom fumbled in her purse for it. "I'm on the same committee as your parents. Are they here already? Of course. My God. I have too many things going on at once."

"What committee?" Jessica asked.

The woman pulled out her phone. "You know. To raise money for the school band trip. Have a good one, guys." She took the call and walked into the café.

Jessica and Albert looked at each other and both laughed.

"Meetings. He was telling the truth!" Jessica said.

"Quick, let's get out of here before they see us." Albert pulled her away.

Jessica said. "Oh my God. This is a relief."

"I totally assumed," Albert said. "And I'm supposed to avoid assumptions."

"What? Who said that?"

"My—my grandma," Albert said quickly. They turned back toward the park. "She's always giving me words of wisdom like *Don't assume! Don't assume!*" Albert's phone buzzed. He read the text.

*For heaven's sake! I'm not dating Sam. He's great, but not my type. We'll talk about this later.*

"One hundred percent total relief!" Jessica said. "But I'm sorry I got you into all this over nothing."

He shrugged and smiled. "It's okay. I'll just tell my mom it was your fault."

They took the widest path that ran through the park so they had room for him to skate and her to skateboard as they continued to talk.

"I'm kind of upset with myself, though," Albert confessed. "Because I was trying to avoid assumptions."

"Some assumptions are wrong, but some assumptions are right," she said. "You kind of don't know until you know." She glided next to him. "Tell me an assumption about me and I'll tell you if you're right."

Albert smiled. "Okay. I assume you love chocolate."

"Not fair. You know that's a fact."

"Okay," Albert said. "I assume you are a deep person."

She stopped. "Why?"

Albert stopped, too. "Because when you were in the fifth grade and Ms. Holly showed us that NASA animation about black holes, you said, 'Sometimes I think I can feel a black hole in my soul.'"

Her eyes widened. "You remember that? I was so embarrassed that day."

"You had just gotten a haircut."

Her smile grew. "You remember everything?"

"I was kind of amazed by you," he said. "I wasn't sure exactly what you meant about having a black hole in your soul but at the same time I felt exactly the same way."

"I remember that day," she said. "I blurted out that thought about the black hole and I remember everybody in class was staring at me like I was crazy—except you." Her eyes softened. "You were looking at me like—I don't know—I could just feel this connection. Like you understood."

"As soon as you said it, I could relate to it. I don't know. Ever since I can remember, I've felt this huge kind of energy inside me. Sometimes it's negative and sometimes it's positive. When it's negative, it makes me feel separate and alone. But when it's positive..." He wanted to say *When it's positive, it's the ahn.*

"When it's positive, it makes you feel connected," she said.

Albert looked up. "That's it."

"When it's negative, it sucks all the energy out of you," she said. "But when it's positive, it gives you more energy than you feel like you can hold."

Like those invisible threads that connected him to his Zeenod teammates, he could feel invisible threads of positive energy running between Jessica and him. It was also like the invisible threads that connected birds and trees and humans. He wasn't sure what to call it in English. He flashed back to the third lesson from Kayko—sending ahnic energy outward—and how simple it was. Send kind thoughts outward. *May you be well. May you feel joy.* He remembered how amazing he'd felt when he had sent those thoughts to Jessica and Trey at the band concert and it had resulted in a positive ripple effect. That connection was the ahn.

"And here's the other thing I've been realizing," he said, encouraged to go on. "It's something you can create in either a negative or positive way. If you send out negative energy, you create more negative energy because people respond negatively, and—"

"And when you send out positive energy, you create more positive energy because people respond positively," Jessica added.

"Exactly!"

She smiled. "Well, Albert Kinney, I think we've discovered the meaning of life or something."

He laughed. They had reached the edge of the park, where their paths home went in opposite directions.

"Let's agree to stop worrying about our parents," she said.

"Done," he said.

"I don't think Trey is using that board I loaned him. Get it from him and bring it next time. I'll teach you some tricks."

He bowed. "Yes, ma'am."

She laughed. "Skateboarding is more fun than jumping into freezing-cold water."

"You're never going to let me forget that," he said.

"See you later, Albert!" She waved and was off.

All the way home, Albert felt a kind of lightness of spirit that he hadn't felt in ages. And then, as soon as he got home, he received a message.

*Albert, this is Lee. Mehk contacted me and told me about his plan to release Zeenod prisoners. I am contacting Zeenods who are living on other planets to tell them about the uprising. We are developing a plan to support the prison breakout. With this final push, we will have our best chance to free Zeeno. We have been spying on the Tevs and heard they are planning an abduction right before the final game. Giac is working to cloak your ITV, but be on guard, Albert. You are in grave danger, but I know you can succeed. On a happier note, Tackle is well. He says he is looking forward to enjoying a carrot with you soon.*

Albert smiled. Lee and Mehk and Tackle and Ennjy all working together! This was amazing. And on top of that, his friendship with Jessica was back on track and his worries about his mom and Mr. Sam were gone.

He got to work, studying the johka tournament guide, learning everything he could learn about what to expect on Tev. The first practice was on Monday, and he was determined to be ready.

A few minutes later, a car pulled into the driveway. He could tell by the banging sounds in the kitchen that Erin had headed straight there and was raiding the cupboards for snacks. There was a knock on his door, and his mom's voice came.

"Albert? Can I come in?"

Albert tucked his Z-da back under his shirt and grabbed the history book that was sitting on his desk. "Sure."

She walked in with a funny smile on her face. "Okay, Albert. What's this about me dating Mr. Sam? Gabby's mom said you and Jessica were outside Buzzy's."

Albert felt his face get hot. "Do we have to talk about this?"

"I don't want you to be anxious!"

"I'm not anxious anymore."

"Were you and Jessica thinking—"

"We just don't want to be, like, brother and sister all of a sudden."

His mom laughed. "Well, I'm not dating Sam, and I promise that if I do start dating someone, I won't keep it a secret. Okay?"

He nodded.

"Mom!" Erin shouted from the kitchen. "Can I make brownies?"

Albert's mom gave him a look. "What do I always tell her?"

"Don't scream from ten thousand feet away."

She laughed. "Exactly!" She got up and then paused in the doorway. "Did you get to see Nana before she had to leave?"

Albert shook his head. "But she left me a long message."

"She called me when I was at the gym. She was sorry to leave so abruptly but said it was an opportunity she couldn't pass up."

Albert was silent.

"Anything you want to talk about, Albert? I know you've been tense lately. Was this just it or is there more going on?"

For a moment, he fantasized that he could unload all his worries, but it was impossible. Besides, things were finally looking up for the Zeenods. He just had to get through this next big challenge.

"Well, I know you miss Tackle," his mom said, filling in the silence. "I keep hoping he'll trot home!"

"Yeah, I do miss Tackle," he said. "And I'll miss Nana. I like having her around. But other than that, it's all good. Thanks, Mom."

"Good!" She blew him a kiss and left.

He pulled out his Z-da and got back to work.

# 9.0

Tackle was snoring in the dark when the whirring of a motor forced him awake. The moment he opened his eyes, he was on full alert. Just inches from his face was a drone.

"Net!" a voice from the shadows cried. And before Tackle could jump out of the way, the drone fired. Instantly, Tackle was tightly wrapped. He started chomping and clawing and wrestling to free himself, and then a light switched on.

*Ha! I did it!* Mehk cried out. He turned to the PEER and said, "Hover!" The PEER whirred up to the ceiling and hovered. *Look at that! Brilliant! It's responding to my voice commands.*

*I can see,* Tackle said as his body calmed down. *But did you have to use me as a test subject?*

*Absolutely necessary!* Mehk laughed with relief as he cut the net. *Finally, I got the code right!*

Free, Tackle shook his muscles out and then looked up at the hovering drone. *Got to admit, it's exciting! Now what?*

*We need to let the Zeenods and Lee know. Then we need to go back to the prison and introduce the code to the PEERs.*

Mehk sat down and put in a call to Blocck to make an appointment for the free inspection he had promised. Tackle paced, only half listening, but then he heard Blocck make a terrible request.

"That Zawg you brought with the good nose," Blocck's voice came through the speaker. "I'd like to buy it from you."

Mehk's bem twitched.

"I'll have the money ready when you get here," Blocck added.

Tackle's ears pricked. Day after day, Mehk had been anxious about money. Tackle knew that Mehk craved a big meal instead of the digging through the dumpsters at night for food that others had thrown away. For a moment, Tackle pictured the worst: Blocck would hand over the money, Mehk would take it and run, and Tackle would be stuck in the prison for the rest of his life. *Grrr.*

"Buy the zawg?" Mehk's voice sounded happy. "What a brilliant idea."

The dog's knees shook. Panting, he wanted to say something, but all that came out was a soft, anxious whine.

"But no," Mehk said quickly. "The zawg is not for sale."

As Mehk finished the call, Tackle felt the strength return to his limbs. And then Mehk turned to face him.

*I was afraid you would say yes!* Tackle said.

Mehk crouched and gave the grateful dog a rubdown. *Three months ago, I probably would have.*

*Hey,* Tackle said, looking up at him. *Your eyes…*

*What about them?* Mehk asked.

The botmaker's eyes were changing color. They were turning gold.

# 10.0

When Albert stepped out onto the Tev landscape for his first practice on the dark, hostile planet, he had trouble figuring out what he was looking at.

"They are waiting for you in front of the practice facility straight ahead," Unit K said. "The gold figures on the right are your teammates. The Tev team is there, too. See the silver figures? And there's President Tescorick, President Lat, a Zhidorian official, and members of the press. You have the skills necessary to achieve success, Albert." One of the robot's tentacles lifted in an odd salute.

Albert squinted. They had landed on some sort of runway in this busy Tev city. Between him and the glowing blobs ahead—which he now understood were life-forms—was a long, dark walk, about half the length of a johka field. He was happy to think he would not have to deal with plunges into gryther-infested ice water, but the darkness here on Tev might be worse. It was daytime, but the sky had that blue-black look of midnight. There was a huge array of colorful lights coming from the skyscrapers and the traffic all around, but there were no streetlights.

Albert activated the glow function of his uniform and slowly walked toward the crowd, the gold glow helping only slightly. It occurred to him that, since he couldn't even see well, he could trip, and this thought sent a shot of anxiety through his system.

Within moments, a cloud of glowing blue dots drew toward him and hovered right in front of his face. The scritches! He had read about these. They were bioluminescent gnats that responded to chemical signatures of certain emotions in different ways. If you were happy, they would dance around your feet with pinkish sparkling light. If you were angry, they would swarm over your head and glow in white pulses. If you were anxious or fearful, the scritches would glow blue and buzz around your eyes and ears. They were like shawble broadcasters.

Albert tried to wave away the gathering cloud of blue. Annoying, distracting, and humiliating! Now everybody knew he was anxious. No way to hide your emotions on this planet! And the slightly higher gravity here was definitely something he could feel. Even though he was empty-handed, he seemed to be carrying weights. He was going to get tired more quickly here.

And then he sensed a shifting in the sky. He looked up. Just above the skyscrapers, he could make out the movement of darker shapes. Haagoolts! The blue cloud in front of his face intensified.

He had read that all Tev buildings emitted sonic pulses at just the right frequency to keep the haagoolts from diving down. The sound created an invisible fence to protect the Tevs from the predators. Albert, however, was in an open section, and he wasn't sure if he was safe. He could imagine the Tevs deliberately leaving an Albert-sized hole in that invisible fence and then shrugging innocently when a haagoolt dove down and slurped him up. Pushing himself, he jogged and then ran the rest of the way.

Through the annoying cloud of blue, he swore he could see the smirks on the faces of the Tevs, their coach Hissgoff, President Tescorick, and President Lat. Albert's anxiety morphed into anger. Within seconds, the gnats shifted, flying above him to pulse, their light now white.

Albert's teammates gave him sympathetic looks as he caught his breath and as the reporter drones swooped in to capture the whole scene on camera.

An elaborate welcome ritual began with ridiculous speeches from both presidents about how much they respected their opponents. All lies. The only way Albert could calm down was to not listen to the speeches. So he looked at his feet and chanted silently: I am calm. I am calm. I am calm. Slowly the gnats disappeared. Finally, the ordeal was over. The Tev team marched into their practice facility and the Zeenods headed to theirs.

Just before walking in, Albert turned and looked around. The Tev capital was packed with skyscrapers and traffic, but the colors and lights were different from anything Albert had ever seen in the cities he had visited on other planets. Ordinarily when you looked at a skyscraper you'd see lights in windows, mostly whitish or yellowish light, sometimes the blue from a television. Here, a kind of liquid light danced all over the surfaces of everything. Yellows, reds, blues, greens, purples.

Remembering that Tevs could see in the dark, he turned to the Zeenod closest to him and asked why they put lights on their buildings if they could see them in the dark. "It's all so beautiful," Albert said. "I didn't think Tevs would be into beauty."

"What looks beautiful doesn't necessarily have a beautiful function," Feeb said. "All of these patterns of color and light are messages that are being programmed to appear. The citizens of Tev are constantly seeing messages everywhere they look."

Albert looked up at the front of the practice facility. A series of yellow dots were trickling over the building's surface. "That pattern of dots means something?"

Giac stepped up. "It's a visual-symbol language. Our translation implants are excellent with Tev speech, but we haven't been able to integrate their visual language into our translation implant yet. I've been trying to master the language, though. I believe that what we're seeing right now is a message telling all Tevs to buy tickets for the game and to support the Tev team."

"Advertising!" Albert said.

Giac nodded. "Advertising but much more. The Tev government uses this system to tell its people what to think and how to behave."

A Tev police vehicle went by, blue and purple dashes and dots flickering across the surface. Giac explained, "That one is saying something like this: Tevs deserve the best. Do not buy any product that has not been Tev-approved. Report your neighbors who buy illegal products and you will be rewarded."

Albert looked beyond the vehicle at the vast array of dancing light on the vehicles and the buildings of the street, trying to imagine what it would be like to see so many messages at once.

"And you know that Tevs themselves can change the colors and patterns on their own skin to send messages," Feeb said as they walked in. "The Sñektis have the same ability, and their culture has also evolved to use a visual language as well as a verbal language. On the johka field, they can't change the color of their uniforms, but they can still send messages, according to FJF rules."

Albert remembered the Skill Show on Zeeno and how Vatria had turned herself into a dancing light display. Now Albert realized that the lights weren't random. She must have been reciting a poem or telling a story or singing a song with her skin.

"Remember, there will be no stadium lights on the johka field, Albert," Ennjy said. "When the Tevs and Vatria played against us on Zeeno, their bioluminescence didn't help them. Here in the dark, they will enjoy a great advantage. They'll use their skin to send messages to each other on the field."

"I should learn it!" Albert said.

Giac shook her head. "It's too complicated. Playing without lights will be hard enough. Just focus on the three different glowing colors. Our uniforms and shoes glow gold, Tevs' gear glows silver, and the ball glows purple. According to FJF rules, no one can alter or turn those off during the game."

They walked through the double doors and into the dark space of the johka field. Albert had been prepared for the fact that the Tevs and Vatria were fast—he had seen that ridiculous speed on Zeeno at the first game. But he hadn't realized how many more advantages they'd have here on Tev. Somehow he had to keep from panicking.

"Let's take our regular positions and do some passing drills," Ennjy suggested.

As the glowing ball hovered and the glowing shapes of his teammates spread out on the dark field, Albert flashed back to the nighttime soccer games he had played on Earth. When he and Trey had been in fourth and fifth grade, they'd had regular sleepovers, and in the summer, they had often snuck out at midnight with Tackle to kick the ball around in Trey's backyard. Trey had gotten a glow-in-the-dark soccer ball and glow-stick bracelets for his birthday and they had worn the bracelets around their ankles, which had been so much fun. It also reminded him of "Glow Nights" at the roller rink. Everybody would get to wear glow-stick bracelets around their arms and legs and skate in the dark.

The Tev practice field did look magical, like a party was going on. Because he couldn't see the faces of his teammates, it looked like the glowing purple sphere was being chased by shoes and uniforms that had come alive.

Okay, Albert, he told himself. Have some fun and just play.

# 11.0

Kayko was thrilled to see Mehk and Tackle when they appeared again in her cell. To be safe, she tried to look bored for the "routine" pest inspection, but Mehk noticed that her eyes were changing color.

Swiftly, the botmaker followed the same procedure they'd used before. He docked her PEER outside the door and told Tackle to get to work sniffing. While the dog pretended to sniff for gheet eggs, Mehk quickly sang his news to Kayko. *"Today I will infect the PEERs with a virus that contains a code. This code is set to activate a new protocol on the day of the final johka game. As soon as activation has occurred, each PEER will be programmed to follow the voice commands of whichever Zeenod each is assigned to guard."*

Kayko's eyes widened. *"Genius!"*

*"You will need to lead, Kayko. Command your PEER to open doors and protect you. If the other Zeenods join, the guards will be overpowered. We will be waiting outside."*

"But the guards will call for help," Kayko sang. "The Z-Tev army will arrive. The PEERs can't win against them. We'll be released only to be caught again."

*"We are working on that. My plan is to—"*

The door to Kayko's cell opened and the whoosh of air from the corridor rippled the edges of Mehk's bem.

Kayko's PEER hovered at eye level in the doorway and announced that prisoners must report for the scheduled work session. Bad timing, Mehk thought. Unable to say anything more, he returned to the pretense of inspecting the cell for gheets.

Kayko stood and—without looking at Mehk or Tackle—walked out the door. Mehk watched as all the imprisoned Zeenods walked down the hallway with their PEERs buzzing overhead. After making their fake-inspection rounds, they knocked on the door of the office of PEER repairs. "Final check for pests," Mehk said to the service technician. "Please step out so my zawg has room."

Tackle barked for good measure, and the technician stepped out. Trotting in, Tackle sniffed, and Mehk followed, closing the door behind. As soon as they had their privacy, Mehk sat down at the technician's main computer, called up the program that communicated protocols to every PEER, and secretly modified the code.

*Success!* Mehk exclaimed. *Unfortunately, we can't test it now. All we can do is hope that when the protocol is activated on game day, it will actually work.*

*If it doesn't?* Tackle's forehead wrinkled.

*Let's not think about that,* Mehk said.

As they were leaving, they heard a disturbing conversation between Blocck and a guard. Mehk stopped, pretending to look for something in his bag, and listened to them.

"An interception of the ITV is planned the night before the game," Blocck was saying. "We can expect that Kinney will—" With the eye in the back of his head, Blocck noticed that the exterminator and his zawg were standing nearby.

"Any gheets?" Blocck asked.

"Completely gheet-free," Mehk said. He held out his phone. "Can I get you to tap me a good rating, sir? You are known as the best warden in the business and that would mean a lot!"

Blocck tapped the ratings bar on Mehk's phone. "Change your mind and want to sell that thing?" Blocck gestured at Tackle.

"No, sir!" Mehk laughed. "But thanks for your offer."

As soon as the two were safely out of sight, they stopped and breathed a sigh of relief. Then Mehk sent a message to Ennjy.

*I heard Z-Tevs talking about an interception of an ITV the night before the game. I heard this rumor before. I believe they're planning to kidnap or kill Albert when he takes off for Tev. Can you cloak Albert's ITV so that they can't locate him?*

Ennjy texted back.

*Kayko and Giac managed to create a successful cloaking situation only once before. And now the Z-Tevs have made it even harder for us to get access to technology. But Giac is working on it. I will warn Albert again at the next practice. Thank you. We are more hopeful than we have been before.*

*Our team is strong. Our former Star Striker Lee has taken great risks and is doing more than we could have dreamed to help us. And now we have you on our team, too. We are grateful to be working with you.*

Mehk read that last line several times, noticing that it made a spot inside his chest feel warm. A good feeling.

*What now?* Tackle asked.

Mehk's eyes flashed. *We're going to the next prison. We'll offer a free inspection. Nobody will turn down a free inspection, especially when we have a high rating from Blocck! We're going to as many prisons as possible between now and game day. The only way to prevent the army from capturing Kayko and the Zeenods from this prison is to have multiple breakouts happening at the same time.*

*I can't wait to see what the army does when it is called in different directions at the same time!* Tackle said. *They won't know where to go. Brilliant!* He jumped up, put his paws on Mehk's chest, and gave his cheek a huge lick.

"Disgusting," Mehk said, wiping his face.

But Tackle could see that the botmaker was smiling.

136

# 12.0

Each day passed slowly. To train for the heaviness of the higher gravity, Albert walked with weights whenever he could. And he tried as often as possible to sneak into the backyard at night and kick the soccer ball around, just to get used to playing in the dark. But without Tackle, his sessions were all work and no fun.

The practices on Tev were tense and exhausting, too—even with his recovery time in the hygg. Every little movement made him tired. Fatigue and tension were even taking a toll on the Zeenods. Worried that they were being spied on, the team hardly talked during practice. That, along with the higher gravity, made each practice seem to last ten times too long.

Ennjy, noticing Albert's fatigue, sent him home with one final audio lesson. After dinner on the evening before the big szoŭ, Albert sat on his bed to listen.

*Welcome to the ninth lesson: Know your why. Take a few moments to focus on your breathing and to be present, and we will begin.*

Albert took a deep breath in, and then Erin burst into the room.

"Look at this, Albert! Brittany posted a fake picture of herself in Miami!" She held out her phone. "She's pretending she got to go to this big tournament, but she didn't go! She put her body in the picture! Can you believe it? She makes me so mad. I want to—"

"Erin!" Albert snapped. "Stop obsessing about Brittany! It's all you do. Tell her you don't like the way she operates and quit gymnastics!"

Erin closed her mouth. Tears welled in her eyes and she turned abruptly.

Albert felt a twinge of guilt, but, really, Erin was being annoying. He had important, life-or-death issues to deal with. He got up, locked his door, sat back down and took a breath.

*Many tasks are hard. If you are facing a difficult task, focusing on how difficult or undesirable or tiring the task is will only make the task harder. Instead, remember why you are doing the task. Knowing your why can provide you with the energy you need.*

He let out the breath he had been holding.

*Imagine you are about to do a chore that you dislike doing at home or at school. Think of a chore now.*

Albert closed his eyes and thought about taking out the garbage.

*While you are picturing yourself doing the chore, imagine that all you are thinking about is how much you dislike the task.*

Albert took in another breath. As he imagined himself lifting the trash bag out of the kitchen trash container, he could smell the stinkiness of the trash. It was raining out and he had been comfy and cozy in his room and now he had to go outside. What a pain.

*Now ask yourself: Why do you need to do this task?*

Albert considered the question. If I didn't take out the garbage I would get yelled at, he thought.

*You might be tempted to think of a superficial reason. Try to think of the real reason that you need to do this task.*

The real reason? Albert thought. What would Nana say if he asked her why he had to take out the trash? He could almost hear her voice. *Albert, if you don't take out the garbage, the kitchen will turn into a dump and an army of rats will move in. Everybody in the family has jobs to do, kiddo, and this one isn't such a big deal. If you won't do it, your mom will have to and she's already doing a lot. So just do it.*

*Once you have remembered the real reason, now go back and imagine the scene, but this time imagine that, while you're doing it, you're remembering the why.*

Albert closed his eyes again. Yes, the trash was stinky as he lifted the bag out of the kitchen trash container and tied it up. Yes, it was raining out, but getting a little wet wouldn't kill him. He imagined his nana smiling as he walked out to toss the garbage in the can. Done!

*Knowing your purpose can help. Take a moment to reflect.*

Albert thought back to the game against the Gaböqs. He remembered how anxious he had been at the opening ceremony. But then, when Albert had seen the crest of Zeeno, with the image of the planet's most beautiful features—the vacha tree, the ahda bird, the zee—his will to restore Zeeno to the Zeenods had been renewed. He had remembered the why then and it had helped.

He pulled out his notebook. Not that long ago, he had written down six things he had learned from Kayko. Now he had three things he had learned from Ennjy to add.

7. *Let negative thoughts come and go without reacting.*
8. *Avoid assumptions.*
9. *Remember the why.*

Feeling better, he went to the kitchen to treat himself to dessert. His mom was mopping the kitchen floor.

"Erin dropped a bottle of orange juice," she said. "She tried to clean it up but then she accidentally knocked over the bucket. She's really upset about something. Go see what's wrong, Albert."

From the top of the stairs, he could hear Erin crying. And as he walked down, the crying stopped. His little sister's old fairy-tale play tent was zipped up tight, but he could hear her sniffling inside.

"Erin, are you upset because I yelled at you?" he asked. "I'm sorry. Come out."

Silence.

"I agree that it was weird for Brittany to post a fake picture," Albert said. "She's probably trying to make people jealous."

Silence.

Albert sat down and unzipped the tent. Erin's red face appeared for a second, and then she zipped it back up.

"Erin, remember when we had that talk right before—" He stopped. He had been about to say, "right before my first johka game against Tev." Quickly he corrected himself. "Right before midnight on your birthday? Mom got mad at us for fighting and we had that talk in Nana's room."

"I remember," Erin said.

"You told me you were under a lot of pressure with your gymnastics team. You said you felt sick whenever it was time for a meet. I asked you if you wanted to quit and you said you were afraid to quit and you were afraid to keep going."

"I remember," she said again.

"And then just a few weeks ago, you faked that twisted ankle to get out of practices and—"

She unzipped the tent. "I wasn't faking. It hurt!"

Albert smiled. "Really?"

She flushed. "Okay. Maybe I was faking."

He shrugged. "Maybe you should quit."

"Quitting is a sign of weakness," she said quickly.

"Who says?" Albert asked.

"Brittany has a poster that says that on the wall above her bed."

Albert sighed. "Quitting before you even try is one thing, but you have tried, Erin. You have been trying for six years already and you're only eleven years old! Why are you on the gymnastics team?"

"Because Brittany says—"

"No," Albert interrupted. "No Brittany. Why are you, Erin, on the team?"

"Because it's the team that wins the most medals. And I have to be on that team now if I'm going to be a star."

"Is that really why you're doing gymnastics? Because you want to be a star?"

She looked at him. Her eyes were still puffy from crying. "Isn't that what I'm supposed to want?"

He took a breath. "What's the real why?"

"Because I'm good at it?"

"You are good at it, but just because you're good at something doesn't mean you should do it. What's your real why?"

"I don't think I have a real why," Erin said. "When we were in kindergarten, Brittany signed up for gymnastics and told me it would be fun. I asked Mom to sign me up. And that's it."

"Okay," Albert said. "If you quit, why would you quit?"

"Why quit?" She looked at Albert. "Because I think I would be happier if I didn't have to go."

Albert smiled. "That's an important why! Okay. So imagine it's a Saturday afternoon. What would you like to do? If you could choose to do anything, would you choose gymnastics?"

She swallowed. "Mom would freak out if I quit. She—"

"That's an assumption," Albert stopped her. "And it's not an answer. If you could choose to do anything, what would you do? I mean, there's nothing wrong with gymnastics. But maybe you're just burned out. You've been doing it and only it nonstop for years and you're only eleven."

Erin smiled. "You know what I was thinking?"

"What?"

"It might be fun to try soccer," she said.

"You're kidding!" He smiled. "Okay. You and me. Right now. Let's grab a ball and go out and—"

She jumped out of the tent and was up the stairs before he could finish the sentence. They set up goals and squared off in the backyard for one-on-one in the growing darkness. "This feels good!" Albert said. He remembered something Nana had always said about how if you're not paying attention, you can miss an opportunity for joy. *If you're doing something you love, remember that it's something you love doing,* she would say. Training and playing were sometimes grueling, but he loved the game, and when he remembered that, he played better and felt better.

Although it grew harder to see as their game went on, Erin's smile never left her face. And then, after they were played out, Erin asked him to help her explain to their mom why she wanted to quit gymnastics.

"I get it," their mom said. "I sensed that you weren't happy, but you kept insisting you wanted to keep doing it."

"So it's okay if I quit?" Erin's eyes welled with tears.

"Honey! Yes, of course." She pulled Erin in for a hug.

"Albert helped me figure all this out," Erin said through her tears, still holding on tight.

Over Erin's shoulder, Albert's mom gave him a grateful smile. The whole thing felt right.

"Nana would love this," Albert said.

His mom laughed. "We'll have to tell her all the details."

After Erin and his mom had gone to their bedrooms and Albert had gone into his, an unexpected heaviness settled over him. It took him a while to realize what was going on. While Erin was entering into a less complicated phase of her life as a young athlete, he was about to enter into the most complicated and final phase of his. Now the life-and-death risk of what he was about to do hit hard.

His mind went through the steps of the journey he was about to take. If he made it safely to Tev, this would be the most dangerous game of all. If anything went wrong with the prison breakout, the Tevs and Z-Tevs would certainly punish Kayko and Mehk and all the Zeenods and Tackle and Lee and Albert, too. For a revolution this big, the punishment would be sure to be death.

Death.

He got up and looked at himself in the mirror and a wave of sadness and panic swept over him. He couldn't imagine not being alive, couldn't imagine not waking up to a new day or seeing his family and friends or kicking around a soccer ball in the park or eating chocolate or learning how to drive or going to high school or growing up. His hands went clammy, his feet felt unsteady, and the room began to spin.

He sat down on the bed, pulled out his Z-da, cupped his hands around it, and closed his eyes. The solid weight of his Z-da always helped to calm him, helped him to remember his deep connection to his Zeenod friends. The memory of that first glimpse of Kayko and the Zeenods came to him. In his mind's eye he could see them staring at him on the video screen in the ITV. They were leaning toward him, eager to meet him with their broad smiles and their extraordinary color-changing eyes.

He stood and looked at his reflection again. His pulse slowed and his hands relaxed. He took a deep breath and let it out, strength returning to his feet and legs and core. Even by just remembering his friends, he was filled with ahn energy. He wasn't alone. He was part of a team. Even bigger than that. He was part of a movement.

Everything he had learned in his lessons came flooding back.

1. *Acknowledge thoughts and emotions without judgment.*
2. *Send kind thoughts to yourself.*
3. *Send kind thoughts to others—even your opponents.*
4. *Be open to learning.*
5. *The most power and joy come through connection.*
6. *Respond to challenges in positive ways.*
7. *Let negative thoughts come and go without reacting.*
8. *Avoid assumptions.*
9. *Remember the why.*

He leaned into the mirror, pressed his Z-da against his heart, and looked deeply into his own eyes. "This is scary, Albert. But you are a Star Striker. May you bring everything you have learned to this next part of the mission."

He felt ready. Or almost ready. He pulled out his phone and sent three texts.

*Hey Freddy, just wanted to say I'm glad you and Min got together. Sorry about anything I might have done in the past. You are a great guy. I know that if I ever needed anything, I could ask for your help. That's huge. I hope that, in the future, I can be a better friend to you.*

*Trey! I was just thinking about those old night games we used to play in like fifth grade. We've had a lot of fun. Just wanted to say I know you're missing Tackle and I'm hoping he comes back. If he doesn't, I bet it's because he was doing something out there to help someone. You know Tackle. A true hero.*

*Hi Jessica. I wonder what you're doing right now. Eating chocolate? Going for a midnight skate? I'm sitting in my room thinking about the meaning of life. Ha ha. But yeah. I am. So...may you be well, Jessica Atwater. May you feel joy. May you be filled with more positive energy than you feel like you can hold. And may that energy spill out into the world and into the stars and into the universe and create positive energy everywhere. Hope to see you later.*

It was bold. He grinned. Why not? What was the point of holding back just because you assumed the other person would think it was awkward or weird? There was a chance of that, but there was also a chance that Jessica Atwater would think his message was the best thing she had ever read.

He wanted to go into Erin's and his mom's rooms and say goodbye and call his nana, too, but he knew that would make them wonder what was going on. Feeling torn, he stood in the doorway of his room and listened to the silence of the house. He closed his eyes and the silence deepened. Then it came to him—a way to connect with Erin and his mom and even possibly with Nana. He called Nana and it went straight to voice mail. That was okay. He held the phone up and let it record as he began to sing the bedtime ritual that Nana taught them so many years ago, the song that had connected him with aliens from all over the Fŭigor Solar System at the Skill Show before the Jhaateez game. The simple sing-and-repeat song that somehow was so beautiful.

"*Ba da dee,*" he sang, and waited in the dark.

"*Ba da dee.*" Erin's voice was the first to float out.

"*Ba da dee da deee,*" Albert sang.

This time Erin and their mom echoed him. "*Ba da dee da deee.*"

Albert took a deep breath and sang louder, changing the melody and phrase again. *"Ba da dee dum dee da dee dum."*

Erin's and his mom's voices entwined. *"Ba da dee dum dee da dee dum."*

*"Ba da doo ba da dee deee."* Albert felt the familiar bubbling up of joy.

*"Ba da doo ba da dee deee."* They all sang, and Albert could feel their joy, too. They loved each other. They would always love each other.

Just like when he was a little kid, the sounds of their voices made the walls and the ceiling disappear. He knew that Nana would listen to the recording, and when she did the miles between them all would disappear, too.

# 12.1

Mehk and Tackle were chatting as they packed up their gear and began to make their way toward the exit of the largest prison north of the capital, their eleventh success story. The fact that the Z-Tevs and Tevs didn't include Dog in their language-translation implants meant that they didn't have to worry about being overheard.

*Do we have time to do another one?* Tackle asked as they walked down the hallway.

*No, but I'm satisfied*, Mehk said. *When eleven different prisons call for help at the same time, the Z-Tev authorities will be pulled in so many directions, they won't know what to do.*

*I can't wait*, Tackle said. *Let's send a message to Ennjy and Lee as soon as we get back to the apartment. Albert will want to know!*

When they reached the exit, they were surprised to see two fully armed Z-Tev police officers talking with the warden. Tackle smelled Mehk's fear, although the botmaker was smiling.

"Sorry to interrupt your meeting, sir!" Mehk said. "We did find one small nest, but we exterminated it at no charge. We'll just be going—"

"Stop!" the warden exclaimed. The two officers stood, blocking the door.

"Is there a problem?" Mehk asked, sweat beginning to appear on his forehead.

Tackle tensed, feeling his fight-or-flight response kicking in.

"I just got a call from Blocck," the warden said. "He said you've decided to give your zawg to him as a gift, to thank him for all the business he has given you."

Tackle's ears flattened and Mehk quickly protested. "That's not true! This zawg is essential to my—"

"Are you accusing my friend Blocck of lying?" The warden sneered.

"Not—not of lying," Mehk stammered. "A misunderstanding—"

"I have been given instructions," the warden said. "My instructions are to have these fine officers take your zawg to be of service to my friend. Blocck has realized how much he values your zawg and appreciates your gift."

"But—"

One officer shot a net at Tackle, which wrapped around him

instantly. The other officer put his hand on his weapon and glared at Mehk.

"We have an extra prison cell here if you'd like to stay with us," the warden said with a smile. "Or you can just walk out and have a nice day."

*Don't fight,* Tackle said, although the net was so tight he could barely move his mouth. *Too risky.*

Mehk looked down, seeing Tackle's own beautiful eyes through the zawg disguise.

The botmaker desperately wanted to scream at these thugs and free the dog, but Tackle was right. The big day was tomorrow. Neither of them could do anything to risk uncovering the plot. And if they were successful—Mehk could free Tackle after the breakout. So he turned to the warden and smiled. "Of course," he said. "Tell Blocck that I hope he enjoys his gift."

Through the mesh of the net, Tackle watched the botmaker leave.

Quickly, the dog was put into an ITV and taken back to the prison near the capital. Blocck had him delivered into his office, where he was cut loose from the net and shoved into a crate.

Take your own advice, Tackle said to himself. Play it cool, Dog. Don't fight. Don't growl or bite. Just stay alert.

He walked a tight circle around himself, which was all he had room for, and then he lay down as if taking a nap in prison were just fine. Deep inside, he felt the churning of anxiety. He was longing to sit up and howl his heart out, howl loud enough to break open this crate, howl loud enough to break open the doors of this prison.

# 12.2

At midnight, Albert snuck into his backyard. He couldn't count the number of times he had initiated a szoŭ to take him into space. Since the day he had been shown the Star Striker contract and had seen the tournament schedule, he had been thinking about this final game. And now the time had come.

There was no way the Tevs would make this journey easy for him. He wished his first chaperone, Unit B, could be with him. He wished Tackle could be with him. Alone, he took one more look at his house, his yard, his street, the planet Earth, and lifted his Z-da to lips.

The moment he materialized on board the ITV, he tensed, expecting to see Lat or Tescorick or Tev thugs, but there was only Unit K, and with good news, too.

"This ITV has been successfully cloaked."

"That's amazing," Albert said, breathing a sigh of relief and knowing how hard that must have been for Giac to pull off.

They took off, and as soon as the autopilot was set, Albert crawled into his hygg. Hibernating in that lovely hydrating nest was the best possible way to deal with his nerves. And for most of the long journey, Albert was blissfully asleep. But as they entered the Fŭigor Solar System, the ITV's information system interrupted with an alarming announcement. "Tev police vehicle approaching. DREDs on board."

Albert raced to the front observation window. Silently he held his breath and watched as the vehicle came into view. "Can they see us?"

Perfectly calm, Unit K kept one head glued to the controls while the other glanced at Albert. "They would have already fired if they had seen us," the robot said. "Would you like the audio channel open to hear what they are saying?"

"Will that make them notice us?"

"If they are unable to see us, they should be unable to detect that we are listening." Unit K flipped on the audio switch with the tip of a tentacle.

For a minute all they heard was the police chattering about what they had eaten for lunch, but then their police vehicle received a call from another vehicle and Albert was astounded by what he heard.

"The interception of Lee is successful! We have locked onto the target's ITV!"

The sound of Tev cheering came.

"Lee?" Albert shouted. "What's going on?"

"If you remain quiet, our likelihood of hearing what they say will increase," Unit K said calmly.

Albert shut his mouth.

An officer's voice came through. "We could easily eliminate Lee now—"

"No. President Tescorick wants you to remain locked onto the vehicle and set your trajectory to—"

Breath held, Albert waited, but the sound crackled and then faded away as the ITV passed out of range.

Albert's mind was spinning. "Follow them! We need to help Lee!" he shouted. "Can you open the communication channel with Ennjy?"

"Increasing the volume of your voice is not necessary."

"Telling me not to yell is not necessary!" Albert yelled. "I'm anxious! Sometimes when I'm anxious I yell, okay?"

The head closer to Albert nodded and one of Unit K's tentacles worked to open the communication channel.

Ennjy's voice came through. "Albert? We are on Tev. We—"

"Lee has been captured, Ennjy!"

Ennjy groaned. "Lee was headed to Zeeno! We were just communicating and the channel stopped working. We thought the Tevs were targeting you! But they must have discovered that Lee has been communicating with Zeenods on other planets—"

The line went dead.

"Ennjy?"

"The channel has stopped working," Unit K said.

"Are you following the police vehicle?" Albert asked. "We need to follow them!"

"That is not advised."

Albert looked at the head closer to him. "Do you or do you not take orders from me?"

Unit K gave a sharp turn and hit the thrusters at the same time and Albert went flying against the side of the ITV.

"Your seat belt should have been fastened," Unit K said.

If Albert hadn't been so angry and terrified and about to vomit, he would have laughed. Quickly he picked himself up, ran to his chair, and locked himself in. That was one advantage to working with a robot: quick responses. If his pilot had been human, the two of them would have had a conversation about the pros and cons of Albert's request before taking action.

They flew for a while in tense silence, Unit K tapping away at the controls to track and tail the Tev vehicle that had commandeered Lee's ITV while Albert remained frozen, staring at the screen.

"According to my calculations, they are headed to Gravespace GJ1. This is one of Tev's moons and Tev's first gravespace. Rescue mission is not advised."

Albert looked out the window. "A gravespace? That isn't so bad. I mean, there will probably be haagoolts. But they weren't so bad—except that's because I had Tackle—Wait!" Albert turned to face the robot. "Somewhere in your files, do you have the sound of a zawg or a dog howling? If you can make that sound, it will keep the haagoolts away."

One of Unit K's heads nodded. "This sound is available for emitting."

"Then we'll be fine. The cloaking mechanism will keep us from being detected, right?"

"Yes, but once we leave the ITV, we will be exposed."

"Everybody on gravespaces is dead! All we have to do is stay hidden from the crypt keeper and find Lee before the haagoolts do. That shouldn't be too hard. Maybe we'll even meet another zawg like Laika!"

After a few minutes of silent flight, Unit K turned one head to stare at Albert. "Jiggling your legs is a waste of energy."

Albert sighed.

When the robot suggested an energy-building rest in the hygg and promised to wake him if he was needed, Albert agreed. This will be a piece of cake, Albert said to himself as he drifted off to sleep. Or as his friend Doz would say, a piece of cookie.

The next thing Albert knew, Unit K was waking him with a grim announcement. "Lee's ITV is here, but this does not seem to be an ordinary gravespace." They were close to landing and a bird's-eye view of the surface was visible. Expecting to see the simple crypt keeper's building and a collection of crypts surrounded by dumping grounds, Albert was shocked to see the lights of numerous buildings and roads and vehicles coming through a gray fog that appeared to be made of dust rather than water molecules.

"This appears to be a secret Tev military base," Unit K said. "There is no record in the Fŭigor Solar System of a base here on GJ1."

Albert's stomach sank.

"Landing is not advised," Unit K said as they hovered.

Albert stared at the hostile-looking scene below, making out Lee's ITV parked in a lot bordered on one side by a river and another by a high wall.

He remembered what it had been like when his ITV was sent to that black hole. He had been sure he was going to die. And then Kayko and Ennjy had come, not knowing if they could rescue him.

"We have to try," Albert said. "I'll have my Z-da, but you're coming with me."

After they landed between Lee's ITV and the river, Albert prepared. He made sure the glow function of his uniform was turned off and then ordered the robot to turn off all alarms and to speak only in a whisper when no other life-forms were visible. The ITV was not equipped with disguises, but the fog of dust in the air would help, and there were two lightweight gray blankets on board that could be worn as cloaks that would camouflage them. When they believed no one was looking, Albert led the way out of the vehicle. First, they ran over the dusty soil toward Lee's ITV. At a glance, they could see it was empty. So they waited again until there were no Tevs in direct sight and then ran along the river-bank, uphill, toward the rear entrance of the largest building.

The smell wafting up was so terrible, Albert was afraid he would gag. "It's got to be a river of trash," he whispered.

"Would you like me to run a chemical analysis?"

"No! Shh!" Albert shut his own mouth and led the way to the entrance.

Fortunately, the first hallway they came to was empty. Unfortunately, it was lined with doors that led to other hallways.

"Where now?" Albert whispered.

"Stop," Unit K whispered, behind Albert.

Albert turned to see both of Unit K's heads peering at the floor.

"Footprints are visible," the robot said. "This footprint has a Zeenod design. Lee wears Zeenod apparel when traveling in our solar system."

Albert noticed the set of prints with a unique design on the dusty floor. "Brilliant!"

They followed the prints down the hall and were about to turn a corner when they heard noises. They ducked into the nearest doorway, which luckily turned out to be a storage closet. They waited until the sounds had faded, and then they returned. After one more safe turn, they had to rush into another doorway, but this time, they were met by the sight of two guards. Although the backs of the guards were toward the doorway, the eyes in the back of their heads were wide open.

Albert turned, but before he could take a single step, the guards had whirled around with weapons drawn. Albert froze, putting his hands in the air. Unit K, however, went into action. Programmed to protect Albert, the chaperone knocked one guard to the ground with one tentacle while another tentacle reached for a weapon.

In that split second, Albert thought they had a chance, but then the second guard managed to fire a net that immediately pinned the robot's tentacles firmly against their body.

Quickly the second guard jumped up, took away both Unit K's weapon and the portable communication device, and shot a pair of handcuffs around Albert's wrists.

"First Lee. And now it's Albert Kinney!" One guard yelled triumphantly.

As the guards rushed them through another set of doors and down one more corridor, Albert kept hoping they wouldn't notice the Z-da around his neck. But when they reached what looked like a cell door, guarded by two new guards, the first guard noticed and yanked it off.

"They probably thought they could rescue Lee!" one said.

"Ha!" Another laughed and peered at Albert. "You want to find Lee? Now you can all be together! President Tescorick will be delighted."

The cell door was opened and Albert and Unit K were shoved in.

# 12.3

With Unit K next to him, Albert stood in the dark cell, over-whelmed by failure. And then a rustling sound came from the shadow of one corner of the cell. With handcuffed hands he activated the glow function of his uniform, and a warm glow radiated from him.

A figure stepped into the glow, and Albert blinked.

"Nana?" Albert's voice came out in a confused whisper.

His grandmother stood in front of him, also in handcuffs, as shocked to see him as he was to see her. She was wearing the type of smartskin tunic and slacks that are typical on Zeeno. Her round face was flushed and her silver hair was in one long braid. Perhaps, he thought, I'm hallucinating. Or perhaps this is an android created to look like my grandmother?

"Albert! Thank goodness you're wearing your uniform. Activate the blade function of your cleats! I'll show you a trick!"

Stunned and further confused, Albert said the voice command *"Blade,"* and his cleats transformed into the skates he used to carve up the ice on Jhaateez.

"Yes!" his grandmother cried. She crouched down, placed her handcuffs over one blade's tip, and used it like a pick to pop the cuffs, which clanked onto the floor. "Ha!" She opened her arms wide and threw them around Albert. "You all right? Any broken bones?" she asked.

Before Albert could respond, she helped him to remove his cuffs and then cut Unit K loose from the net. One of Unit K's heads swiveled to face Nana while the other kept an eye on the door. With a bow of that head, Unit K said matter-of-factly, "Greetings, Lee. I am Albert's chaperone. We are unharmed."

"But she—she isn't Lee," Albert stammered. "She's my grandma."

"I am both, Albert." Lee smiled and looked at Albert with soft eyes. "I have been both all along."

Albert was speechless.

"To you, I'm Nana, of course," Lee said. "My name is Aileen—you know that. But you probably didn't know that seventy-five years ago, my nickname was Lee. I was twelve and that's when I was recruited as Star Striker for Zeeno."

A rush of thoughts hit Albert all at once. He pictured the johka-din card he had seen for Lee. The fully uniformed and helmeted young athlete in that photograph was his grandmother? Albert had assumed Lee was a boy.

"I kept my identity from you a secret, Albert," Lee said. "I thought it would be too tempting for us to talk about Zeeno on Earth. I thought we would risk being discovered."

"You're Lee?" Albert tried to take it in.

She nodded.

"Lee's identity has been established," Unit K said to Albert, and then the robot turned to Lee and asked, "Are you injured?"

"I am hungry and tired, but no broken bones, thankfully." She turned back to Albert and gave him another hug. "You came to rescue me, kiddo! I should have known." Her eyes brightened. "Do you have your Z-da?"

"They took it."

She winced. "We'll have to get out of here the old-fashioned way and make a run for it."

"Wait," Albert said. "I can't believe all this. You've known that I'm a Star Striker all along?"

"I knew the Zeenods were going to recruit you. I didn't know if you would accept or if you would quit at some point along the way. I didn't want my having been a Star Striker to influence you, so that's also why I kept my identity a secret. I wanted the decision to be yours and yours alone."

Albert's mind raced. "That time when you came to visit me in the medic tent when we played against Tev. And that time when Ennjy took me out of the Jhaateez game and you came to the locker room—"

"Both times I wanted to take off my disguise, but I thought it was for the best to stay hidden."

"Both times, you really helped me," Albert said. "You've given me so much good advice—I mean as Nana and as Lee."

She smiled. "I tried to support you whenever I could in a way that seemed natural."

All the little ways she had helped began to come to him. "The trampoline, which helped me on the zees," Albert said, "and the skates, which helped me on Jhaateez, and the pool, which helped me on Gabōq—those were your ideas."

She shrugged. "I've been so proud of you, Albert, of your willingness to keep trying, your love for your team."

Albert shook his head. "For months, Trey was a robot and you were Lightning Lee and I didn't know. Did you know about Trey?"

"I only pieced it together after Tackle and the real Trey returned," she said. "Mehk created an amazing replica of Trey. That botmaker is a genius. And now, thanks to you and Tackle, he's on our side."

Our side. Albert tried to understand this new image of his grandmother as a Zeenod team member. "Wait," Albert said. "What about your broken hip? Was that real?"

"I did break my hip. And it ended up being a great excuse to keep me at your house."

"You could have had it healed quickly by fehkhatting—"

"I did." Lee grinned. "But I pretended that it was healing slowly—just like you did when you broke your arm before the Jhaateez game."

He smiled. "All those trips where you were supposed to be going to the doctor or to physical therapy?"

"I was scooting away to help the Zeenods in whatever ways I could and then time-folding my returns. Once I knew you had joined the Zeenods, I wanted to stay in Maryland so I could keep a close eye on you and do whatever I could to make your travel to and from the solar system easier. I would often cover for you, Albert."

In the bleak cell, Albert stared at his beloved nana's familiar face. "I can't believe you're Lightning Lee! You played against the Sñekti team and against Vatria's grandfather Paod Skell and you won."

"That was the last game that Zeeno played as a free planet." Her eyes grew moist. "Back then, Albert, it was a lovely time on Zeeno. The trees and birds and zees were all so beautiful! The ahn energy was strong and the Zeenod people were healthy and happy. No one suspected what was soon to come." She took a breath. "After I played that first game for Zeeno, I was hoping to go back and play in the johka tournament the next year, but the Z-Tevs made sure the Zeenods wouldn't qualify to be in the tournament. The Zeenods who escaped to other planets kept trying to warn the entire solar system what was going on, but the Tevs had all the power and covered up what was happening. By the time I was in my twenties, I heard that life on Zeeno had become a nightmare. I began to work secretly for the Zeenods. I moved to a secluded farm in New Zealand to make it easier."

"You started your school? Your nature-education center?"

"That's what you can see, Albert. But behind the little school is a huge, hidden farm. On it, there's a secret bank for Zeenod seeds and a nursery for Zeenod plants and an aviary for ahda birds. I am trying to prevent extinction."

Albert eyes widened. "Were you the secret benefactor who released the blossom petals and the birds for the first-game celebration?"

She smiled. "The Z-Tevs and Tevs were furious! They had no idea where those came from!" Her face grew serious. "Of course what I've done is against the rules. You know that the only things we're allowed to bring from the Fŭigor Solar System back to Earth are our Z-das."

"You're breaking the rules for a good reason."

She nodded. "I'm taking the chance that I will be forgiven and pardoned once the truth about Zeeno is revealed."

"Ennjy said you've been communicating with all the Zeenods on other planets, right?"

"I've been recording statements from Zeenods who have witnessed oppression. And that's not all…" She pulled her long braid around and showed Albert her hair tie with a small decorative button. "This is a micro–video recorder. Secretly, I've been recording what the Tevs and Z-Tevs have been doing." Sadness swept back into her eyes. "You've seen what's happening, Albert. Every Zeenod I knew was either killed or imprisoned or sent to a zone to live, which is basically another kind of prison. The Tevs have to be stopped." She leaned forward. "And now we have the best chance we've ever had. I was on my way to Zeeno for the big breakout."

A chill went through Albert. "Do the Tevs know about the plan?"

"I don't think so," she said.

Albert thought of Kayko and Tackle in prison with all the other Zeenods. "We have to get out of here. I wonder how many Tevs are guarding this place?"

Unit K stepped forward. "According to the data I have been collecting since arriving, I would estimate that there are eight hundred to a thousand Tev soldiers occupying this base here on GJ1."

Lee took a long look at the Zhidorian-based robot. "Maybe this unit can be programmed to help. May I open your control panel? I may be able to adjust your code to help."

One tentacle reached behind to pop open a panel on their

back. "You may adjust the code in whatever way helps to keep Albert safe."

"We have to get out before Tescorick comes," Lee said while she worked. "I heard from one of the guards that before he kills me, he wants to know exactly what is being done to help the Zeenods." She continued to work as she talked. "The Tev guards will never suspect that we've gotten out of our handcuffs or that Unit K has gotten out of the net. So we'll have the element of surprise. I think there are two or three guards assigned to this corridor. If so, we can overpower them and try to find an exit."

Albert was still trying to wrap his brain around what was happening.

"There!" She flipped Unit K's panel shut.

"What did you do?"

"I changed Unit K's tracking protocol," she said. "We'll have to leave Unit K behind, Albert. The Tevs will know that the robot is programmed to track you, but now the robot's system is set to display false tracking coordinates. When the Tevs use this unit's tracking data to chase us, they'll be led in a different direction. By the time they figure it out, hopefully we'll be leaving in an ITV."

Both of Unit K's heads swiveled, one to face Albert, one to face Lee. "Ready," the robot said.

Albert flashed back to the first johka game when Unit B made the sacrifice to save his life. He knew that the two-headed computer standing in front of him wasn't a life-form with emotions and fears, but he still felt compelled to say thanks. "You have been an excellent chaperone, Unit K. Your service will be appreciated."

Unit K bowed.

After talking through a plan for disarming the guards, they were ready. They helped each other to rearrange the handcuffs and the net so that they looked as if they hadn't been removed, and then Albert took his place on the floor by the door and gave Lee the signal.

Lee pounded on the door. "Albert Kinney needs medical help!" she shouted.

The door opened and a guard peered in.

Albert pretended to have fainted, and Lee crouched by his side.

When the guard stepped in to get a better look, Nana pulled him down and grabbed his weapon. Immediately, the other two guards rushed in. Albert tripped one, and with one sweep of a tentacle, Unit K knocked the other against the wall.

Lee fired three nets, one around each guard, and Albert took their weapons. Triumphantly the three rushed out, locking the door behind them.

"We did it!" Albert cried.

Lee hugged him and then turned to the robot. "Do not follow us," she whispered.

Unit K ratcheted into a sitting position, and Lee and Albert took off. Cautiously, they opened the hallway door just a crack and listened. Hearing no one, they crept out to find another long corridor. They rushed down that, passing a garbage chute, hoping to find another set of stairs. As they were about to follow the hallway's curve, they heard voices ahead.

"There's only one way out now," Lee whispered.

Unfortunately, Albert knew exactly what Lee was suggesting. Together, they raced back to the chute marked with the Tev word for trash. Lee opened the chute, and Albert looked down, holding his breath. A mouth of putrid darkness.

The voices ahead grew louder, and Lee said, "Let's go."

Stomach churning, Albert plugged his nose and slid down, the glow of his uniform enabling him to see the walls and ceiling of the tunnel as he plummeted in a spiral. Just when he was beginning to think he wasn't ever going to hit bottom, he spilled out. And then came the shock of water, and worse: when his head popped back up above the surface, he breathed in the most horrible smell. Old bottles and discarded objects floated by.

A river of garbage, Albert thought. Of course the Tevs would dump their trash in their rivers. He gagged and tried to stay calm as his grandmother surfaced next to him.

"You okay, Nana?"

"No broken bones. Whoa. What a smell. Let's remain calm, kiddo. We're not on Gaböq, but there still might be grythers here."

Gently but quickly, Albert turned to face the shore, thinking only of getting out of the filthy water. It was then that he was able to see the scene into which they had splashed.

The huge dark cave into which they had fallen was filled with Tevs. Hundreds of Tevs were standing along the bank of the river, staring at them with their red eyes glowing.

# 12.4

This is it, Albert thought, seeing all those red Tev eyes locked on him. After all the dangerous situations he had gotten into, he had finally reached one he couldn't possibly get out of.

Gently treading the muck next to him, Lee was speechless, too.

"Earthlings?" A Tev closest to the river spoke, the sound of his voice echoing in the high-ceilinged cave.

"What do we do?" Albert whispered.

"I don't think we have a choice," Lee whispered back, and then she spoke to the crowd. "Yes. We are Earthlings. We are unarmed."

Albert followed as she swam to the riverbank, assuming that the moment their hands touched the rocky ledge, they'd be hauled up and handcuffed. Albert's mind jumped ahead, thinking of all the possible ways they might be executed—shot? Hung? Buried alive? Drowned? Fed to a haagoolt?

But as they approached, two Tevs reached out to help them up.

Albert glanced at his grandmother, astonished.

"Who are you and why are you here?" the first Tev asked.

Shocked that they weren't recognized, Albert and Lee looked at each other again. Albert was about to whisper that they should lie when his grandmother bowed. "I am—"

A younger Tev blurted out, "Star Striker Lightning Lee!"

An older Tev female stepped forward. "Lee? Is it true?"

Lee nodded.

Albert assumed they would cheer and pull out their weapons, but instead they stood silent. In that stillness, Albert had a moment to notice their tattered and dirty work clothes and guessed they weren't guards or soldiers.

The older female bowed. "Lee, I was the Tev keeper you played against. What was it, seventy-five years ago?"

Lee struggled to understand, peering at the old Tev. "You're Devrik Tok?"

A genuine smile broke out on the Tev's face. She had the features common to all Tevs: that large, square jaw, batlike ears, and two bold striped markings from her forehead and winding around her mouth. Her eyes, too, were reddish orange with that jagged rectangular pupil. All the Tevs standing in front of Albert had those characteristics, but the way they stood and the expressions on their faces spoke of curiosity and compassion, not hostility.

A younger Tev asked Albert, "Are you Star Striker Albert Kinney?"

Albert nodded, and the Tevs bowed. Quickly a bucket with water was brought and a Tev began to help them to wash away at least some of the foul-smelling muck clinging to them. A lump rose in Albert's throat. "What's going on?" he whispered.

Lee looked astonished, too, and Devrik noticed. "We are not those Tevs," she said, pointing upward. "We are the banished ones."

"Banished?"

Devrik nodded. "After losing that johka game seventy-five years ago, I was forced here as punishment. All my teammates and I were sent here after that loss and have been imprisoned here on GJ1 ever since."

Albert had heard about the severe punishments the Tev leaders handed out to players who didn't succeed, but he had assumed it was an exaggeration.

Lee looked at the crowd. "Are you all athletes?"

Another Tev spoke up. "We are athletes and artists and scientists and Tevs of all professions. We are the ones who didn't live up to the Tev ideal or who opposed the occupation of Zeeno or who refused to turn our neighbors or our family over to the police on false charges or who tried to leave the planet for a better life."

Devrik and many others nodded.

"I assumed all Tevs were oppressors," Albert blurted out.

"We oppose what the Tev leadership has been doing. And we are paying the price. We know that the Tev leadership has kept our imprisonment a secret," Devrik said.

"The Tevs in power are very good at telling stories to cover up the truth," Lee said. "No one sees what is truly happening on Zeeno, and no one sees what's happening here."

All the Tevs nodded. Another Tev stepped forward. "We've tried to escape, but we haven't succeeded. Every day, we work together toward that ultimate goal. And we help each other survive." She looked at her fellow Tevs with affection and then placed her hand on the shoulder of the younger Tev. "New Tevs arrive every year. They bring us news."

"Have you heard that the Zeenods are playing in the first johka tournament since the invasion?" Lee asked. "We are working together with Zeenods and allies to reclaim Zeeno."

Albert nodded. "We have plans to show the solar system what Tescorick and Lat have been doing."

The younger Tev spoke again. "I was sent here just before the tournament started. We are eager to know what has been happening!"

Lee looked at Albert.

Albert was taking a breath, about to speak, when suddenly there was a commotion.

"The guards!" someone said.

Devrik and another Tev threw their cloaks over Albert and Lee and pushed them down. "Routine work inspection," Devrik whispered. "Stay hidden."

Under the thick, smelly cover, Albert froze, heart pounding, listening to the approach of bootsteps on the rocky surface, hoping the guards hadn't yet learned that they had escaped.

What sounded like a dozen guards barked orders and walked around and around. It all sounded routine, but then a loud announcement came through a sound system from above.

"Code X9K2. Code X9K2. Two Earthling visitors are trying to flee and must be apprehended. Inform workers that these Earthlings are criminals and any workers who aid them will be executed."

A tense discussion erupted among the guards, and Albert tried to keep his body from shaking.

Another voice came through. "Guard Unit 43, what is your location?"

A Tev commander standing just a few steps away from where Albert and Lee were hiding replied. "This is Guard Unit 43. We are currently underground at Work Area 561."

"Return to the main floor and take positions for a lockdown. We are tracking the Earthlings' route through the eastern tunnel via their robotic pilot. We have just sent several units to stop them."

Lee's trick was working! If the guards were moving east, they could go west and maybe escape before the guards found out that Unit K was leading them astray.

The footsteps retreated. After a few seconds, the cloaks were removed.

Albert and Lee stood up and gushed thanks to their new friends.

"They said they were tracking you!" the newest of the workers said. "Yet they ordered the guard unit back to the main floor."

Lee smiled. "We played a trick on them with the help of our robotic chaperone."

"Ah!" Devrik's face broke into a grin. "If they're expecting you to go east…"

"We'll go west," Albert said. "But we have to go fast."

Lee nodded and then looked at Devrik. "You have all risked your lives to help us. We will not forget this. When we make it out of here and succeed in freeing Zeeno, we will come back to GJi and help you win your freedom."

Albert noticed his nana had said "when" and not "if." He wasn't as confident, but the whole cavern seemed to lift with hope.

"The fastest way out?" Lee asked.

Albert brightened. "I remember seeing the river of garbage when I landed the ITV. I followed it uphill and saw that the building is built over it. We could make a raft and ride it out on the river! Is that west?" He took a breath, excited by his idea, and looked at the side of the cavern where the river disappeared into a dark tunnel of rock.

"It is west and it is the only way that will lead out of the base." A look came over Devrik and the other Tevs. "But there is one problem. The only way out is through the vikkit nest."

"What's a vikkit?" Lee said.

"I have a feeling we don't want to know," Albert said, fear creeping back in as he stared in the direction of that dark tunnel.

"A vikkit is an amphibious creature that can eject a round globule of a flesh-eating toxin from its mouth. No smartfabric protects against this."

"Great," Albert said. "So, basically, a toxic spitball. And if this lands on us, we die?"

"Your flesh dissolves first, and then you die," Devrik said.

"How big are the globs?" Albert asked

"About the size of your fist," Devrik said.

Lee winced. "Please say there is only one of these creatures here."

"There is only one remaining," Devrik said. "But its nest blocks the only way out."

"You'll need leks," the newest Tev said, and ran to hand them two flat objects that looked like Ping-Pong paddles. "These are the leks from the kitchen used to stir the largest kettles. We collect them when they are thrown out. If you strike a globule, it will evaporate, and these are good for striking."

Imagining a toxic ball of spit coming at him, Albert held his paddle and took a swing.

"We can do this, Albert," Lee said. "I like your idea of a raft, so let's—"

"No. You can't ride the river," Devrik said. "The vikkit can swim fast and would overtake you. You have to fly."

At that, another Tev pulled a small flutelike object from his pocket and blew. Albert and Lee heard only the sound of air rushing through it, but then they both sensed a rustling sound from above and they looked up.

A stain on the broad cavern ceiling began to shift. And then, to Albert's horror, the shape peeled itself down from the ceiling and stretched its wings. They were looking up at the gray underbelly of a haagoolt! There were the strange slits and the eyes that protruded out and swiveled down.

Instantly Albert recalled the long tongue that had emerged to snatch Tackle by the tail, and he felt like he was going to throw up. Lee, too, was panicking, lifting her lek like a weapon.

"Don't worry!" Devrik assured them. "We have befriended this haagoolt. Its tongue was shot by a Tev several years ago and it almost died. It cannot digest life-forms anymore. But we taught it to drink from the river and it receives enough nourishment to exist."

Trying to control their impulses to run, Albert and Lee stood next to each other and watched the raylike creature swoop down and land on the surface of the water, where it floated close to the bank, wings outstretched. The creature's size was astounding—it reminded Albert of a giant manta ray—and its beautiful burgundy color was magnificent. Several Tevs leaned over to pet the creature. Albert flashed back to the long walk he and Tackle had to make on GJ7 and how nauseating it had been to walk over all the haagoolts that had fallen dead.

"You can ride the haagoolt out, following the river," Devrik said. "Your first task will be to get through the vikkit nest. Don't worry about the haagoolt getting hit. They are immune to the toxin. So just protect yourselves. Your second task will be to slide off the moment you emerge into daylight. Guards routinely shoot haagoolts. Your third task will be getting to your ITV without being captured again or shot. Every week, one of us volunteers to try escaping in the hopes of leaving this moon and telling the story of what is happening here."

Lee and Albert said nothing. They both knew that the rest of the Fŭigor Solar System believed the moon was uninhabited, which meant that their brave warriors had not made it off the moon. They had one advantage: Albert's cloaked ITV, waiting for them.

Lee looked at Albert. "Three little tasks, kiddo. Ready?"

Albert swallowed down the dread and nodded. They had no choice.

Devrik showed them how to crouch down and climb from the bank onto the haagoolt's wing and then to crawl to the center of its back, harder to do with a lek under one arm. Up close Albert could see that the burgundy color was produced by long, slender feathers.

"Your best position is to kneel side by side. Hold on with one hand by digging under the feathers and grabbing hold of the skin. It won't hurt the creature."

Kneeling next to Lee, Albert gritted his teeth and stuck his hand under the feathers and grabbed a handful of clammy, cold skin.

"Ready?" Lee asked.

"Ready," Albert said.

The same Tev who'd called the haagoolt blew the whistle again, and before Albert and Lee could turn and say goodbye, they jolted up and forward.

Albert almost toppled off, and quickly tightened his grip.

In an instant, they shot into the mouth of the tunnel. Albert gasped, sure that the haagoolt wouldn't fit, but it adjusted its wing movements. Albert and Lee ducked as they sailed through.

The tunnel twisted and turned, so all they could do was hold on and keep their heads down and try not to gag at the intense smell. And then they began to see a change in the light ahead.

"I think we're coming to another cavern or a bigger part of the tunnel," Lee said. "Get ready."

"This thing flies fast enough," Albert said. "Maybe we'll fly through so fast the vikkit won't even see us."

Sure enough, in just a few seconds, the narrow tunnel opened up and they entered a cavern about forty feet by forty feet. No creature in sight. He could even see daylight through an opening on the other side. Maybe the thing was asleep, Albert thought as the haagoolt rose higher.

And then, "Look out!" Lee yelled.

Albert's head snapped in the direction Lee was facing just in time to see a creature emerge from the river and climb onto the wide, rocky ledge ahead. The fat thing had smooth, translucent skin. It was the shape of a salamander but was the size of a great white shark, which meant that it took up almost half the cavern space. Albert was thinking that as long as it stayed down there, it wasn't so bad, when the vikkit suddenly rose up on its hind legs, making a loud ratcheting sound as its vertebrae locked into place.

Suddenly the lek in Albert's hand seemed ridiculous. They needed huge shields and weapons to fight back, not Ping-Pong paddles!

Instinctively the haagoolt turned and flew high, and both Albert and Lee craned back to look. As the vikkit glared at them, a tongue shot out from its huge mouth and licked each of its eyeballs. In the next split second, the mouth puckered. *Pshoo! Pshoo! Pshoo! Pshoo!* One at a time, four balls of rubbery, yellowish slime came flying toward them.

Instinctively the haagoolt dove downward and Albert and Lee ducked. Albert heard the projectiles whiz over their heads and then smack the wall on the opposite side. *Bam! Bam! Bam! Bam!* Vaporized.

The haagoolt turned sharply to fly toward the exit. Just as Albert was beginning to feel relief, the vikkit raced over to block the opening. From there, it shot four more globs. *Pshoo! Pshoo! Pshoo! Pshoo!*

Here they couldn't duck or dive. Both Albert and Lee lifted their leks. *Bam! Bam!* Lee got two. *Bam!* Albert got the third smack in the center. *Bam!* He nicked the fourth one with the tip of his lek just enough to vaporize it, too.

"We did it!" Albert yelled as the haagoolt veered up and away. For the next minute, the haagoolt made a series of dizzying darts and dives as the vikkit shot another round. The elation Albert had felt at getting his first hits evaporated. "How are we going to get out if it stays there?" he cried.

"I think we have to fly *toward* it and chase it away from there," Lee said. "I'll steer." She shoved her lek under one knee, grabbed hold of the haagoolt's skin with both hands, and steered the creature in a wide turn.

*Pshoo! Pshoo! Pshoo! Pshoo!* Four more globs sailed toward them. It was up to Albert to deal with them. He tightened his grip on the haagoolt with one hand and on the lek with the other. *Bam! Bam! Bam! Bam!* He stayed steady and nailed them all.

"Nice job!" Lee exclaimed.

Albert took a breath.

Lee steered the hagoolt in a wide circle and then faced the vikkit directly.

"Move!" Lee shouted. "Move, sucker!"

The cheeks of the huge, blubbery thing quivered. Its mouth puckered up.

"It's not moving!" Albert yelled.

*Pshoo! Pshoo! Pshoo! Pshoo!*

Four globs came right at them. Lee grabbed her lek and held it up like a shield just in time to catch one of the globs right in the center. The second was aimed too low and hit the haagoolt between the eyes. The third and fourth came at Albert, and he wound up and swung. *Bam! Bam!*

Success! But...they were going to crash right into the thing's head!

"Brace me!" Lee shouted.

Albert threw the arm holding the lek around her legs and tightened his grip on the haagoolt, while Lee stood. As hard as she could, she threw the lek at the vikkit. The paddle sailed like a javelin and—*smack!*—it punctured one eye.

"*Aaaaiiiii!*" The vikkit screeched and dropped down to wrestle the lek out of its eye. Immediately, the haagoolt flew over the top of its head toward the tunnel opening.

"Duck!" Albert cried, pulling Lee down just in time. Albert felt the razoring claw of the rocky doorway along his back, and then they were through.

The sight of daylight and the river and the ITVs in the distance seemed like a dream, and then the haagoolt turned sharply toward the riverbank and suddenly flipped upside down. Albert and Lee both screamed and fell, landing on the bank.

In a flash, the haagoolt was slipping back into the tunnel and was gone.

"I'm okay. You okay?" Lee asked.

"I think so," Albert said and felt along his back, expecting a gash. "That was close." He checked Lee's back, too, but their smartskin fabric had protected them.

"Uh-oh," Lee said, staring at the building.

Albert looked. Two Tev guards by the doorway were facing the other way but looking at them with their rear eyes. Those eyes!

"Run to your ITV!" Lee whispered.

Albert stumbled to his feet and began to run, assuming she was right behind him.

A shot fired. He ducked down and ran in a zigzag, panicking when out of the corner of his eye he saw Lee running toward her ITV.

"It's this way!" he yelled.

Their only hope was to make it into the cloaked ITV. Why wasn't Lee following him? Shots were firing, and he kept expecting to feel the hit or hear her cry.

An alarm sounded. More guards were coming.

Set to recognize his face, the ITV hatch whooshed open as soon as Albert was within range. In that moment, Albert could see the interior of his spacecraft. Almost out of breath, he darted inside and turned. Lee was nowhere in sight. In the distance, he watched four Tev fighter vehicles rise and head his way. They had gotten a glimpse of the spacecraft's interior, too! He had to close the door and move or they'd blow him to bits.

Quickly he closed the hatch and sat at the controls. He rose and darted to the side.

One of the vehicles aimed where Albert's vehicle had just been and—*Boom!*—fired a missile that went whizzing past. Albert had moved just in time.

Through the window, he spotted Lee climbing aboard the ITV she had been captured in. Immediately, a Tev vehicle flew toward her. The others followed. She was luring them away so Albert could escape! Albert's heart jumped into his throat.

He could see one of the vehicles swivel to prepare an attack on Lee's ship. He had to save her! Quickly he swerved toward her ITV and hovered above it.

Quickly, he issued a voice command: "Computer, activate the szoŭ for Lee." He held his breath. She was right below. He knew the computer could detect her location. Come on! Come on!

*Boom!* A short-range DRED launched. Through the window, Albert could see it was aimed right below him at Lee. He had to move! Where was she? Why wasn't she appearing?

And *Boom!* The explosion below sent Albert's ship flying upward and sent Albert flying, too. He hit the ceiling and then fell to the floor. For a moment, he wasn't sure if his ship had been hit. His ears were ringing; everything was spinning; and then, in front of his eyes, specks of color materialized and his beloved grandmother's shape took form.

"Nana?" he whispered, thinking he was seeing her ghost. And then she rushed toward him and locked him in the tightest hug.

"You—you were going to sacrifice yourself so I could escape," Albert managed to stammer.

She pulled back to see him. "I thought if we split up, you'd have a better chance. But you saved me, kiddo, you did it!" She beamed. "Now, let's get out of here!"

# 12.5

Just a few minutes after Albert and Lee's ITV exited the crossfire, they overheard a message being broadcast.

"Lee's ITV destroyed by DRED. Albert Kinney has escaped in a cloaked vehicle."

"The Tevs and Z-Tevs think you died!" Albert said.

Lee's eyes lit up. "Let's keep them thinking that!" she said. "I'll be safe if they aren't looking for me. We need to get you to Tev for the game, Albert. Set the trajectory! We need to keep this plan moving forward. When you arrive, pretend you're sad that I died. Focus on the game. Play that game with everything you've got."

"But what about you?"

"Leave that to me. Hop in your hygg and get some rest before the game. You'll need it. I'll pilot the ship."

She was right. He desperately needed to rehydrate and rest if he was going to play his best. He activated the hygg and was about to get inside when he turned and looked back. There was his grandmother with her long gray braid, his grandmother who was a former Star Striker and now a crucial part of the Zeenod revolution. "Wait—Nana—I have so many questions. Were you called Lightning Lee because you were fast?"

She smiled. "I was fast."

"You must have been an amazing soccer player."

"Like you, Albert. You are an amazing player."

"But there are so many amazing players—I know I'm not the best."

"What does the best mean, Albert? Who is the best?"

"Someone who doesn't need so much training! Someone who doesn't make so many mistakes or get scared."

"Skills like speed and strength and agility are important," Lee said. "But there is no such thing as the perfect player, Albert. Yes, you have gotten scared. Yes, you have made mistakes. But you've proven over and over that you can admit your shawbles and grow and learn. And you also have the ability to connect, Albert. That's not something everybody is open to learning about. What the Zeenods saw in you—and in me, too—was an openness to the ahn."

"And you've been helping the Zeenods ever since?"

"Trying."

A new thought occurred to Albert. "Did my father? Did he know? Was he—?"

"Your father wasn't in the right time or the right place to be recruited, although he could have been a Star Striker. He never knew about my situation. Keeping it from him was very difficult, but I gave him a normal life."

"So what I thought happened to him did happen to him? He had an ordinary heart attack?" Albert asked.

She nodded. "Having him die at such a young age was a shock and so hard for all of us. But I know that if he were here, he would be very proud."

The look she gave him made him feel like he was going to cry.

Quickly, she swept him up in a hug. Albert squeezed her back, feeling the ahn flowing between them.

She pulled away and her look of sadness deepened. "Listen, I have discouraging news about Tackle. I didn't tell you before because I didn't want to overwhelm you."

Albert felt his heart thump against his chest.

She went on. "I heard from Mehk that Blocck kept Tackle in prison on Zeeno."

Tackle, a prisoner? Albert stood up. "I have to go to Zeeno and get him out!"

She put a hand on his arm. "We each have a job, Albert. You know Tackle. He will find a way. And Mehk is our ally now. He will help. Your job is to win that game." Her smile was gentle.

"I'll wake you when we get there. I'll time it so we can beam you directly onto the johka field. We don't want to give the Tevs any chance to find and assassinate you before the game starts."

Albert looked at her. She was the same Nana, but she wasn't the same at all. "Out here, I feel like I should call you Lee instead of Nana. Would that be weird?"

She smiled. "Out here, kiddo, weird is normal."

# 13.0

The moment Albert appeared on the johka field during the warm-up, his team went crazy. When they had heard about Lee's supposed death and when Albert hadn't shown up for the pre-game events, they had assumed he had been killed, too. Desperately, Albert wished he could tell the truth about Lee, but Lee had thought it safer to keep quiet. They were devasted about Lee, but jubilant to have Albert back.

Before the game rituals started, reporters crowded around both Albert and Vatria for final interviews. The sky above was dark, but Albert recognized the glow of the moon known to all as the uninhabited Gravespace GJ1 and thought with wonder about how he and Lee had just escaped from there with their lives intact. What an astonishing whirlwind!

"We can see that you're anxious, Albert Kinney," the first reporter said with a snide smile. "What chance does Zeenod have to win?" The video drone hovering over her shoulder zoomed in for a close-up.

Albert stood on the threshold of the field with a cloud of blue scritches hovering around his ears and eyes. He wanted to swat them away, but he knew that would just make him look ridiculous. The only way to make them go away was to calm down his emotions, and he was having a hard time gaining control.

The Tev stadium was beautiful in its strange, eerie way. It didn't have Jhaateez's geodesic diamonds and icy prisms of light or the simple beauty of Zeeno, but the darkness was dramatic. Forcing his attention back to the interview, he said, "We don't have a *chance* to win. We *will* win."

The reporter laughed. "Hard with no fans in the stands. Such a shame. Everyone thought at least some Zeenods would come. Do you think they've given up on their home team?"

Albert looked out. Tev fans made up the vast majority in the stands. Like the players, they wore luminescent colors to match their planets' chosen uniform colors. Tevs and Z-Tevs in silver, Gaböqs in red, Yurbs in brown, Sñektis in teal.

Albert was dying to tell the reporter directly why there were no Zeenods on Tev and to explain how innocent Tevs were being imprisoned on Gravespace GJ1, but he knew it wasn't the right time. Instead he gestured up at the smaller blocks of purplish blue in the stadium. "See? The Jhaateezians are here to support us. And look. Our friends from Liöt, Fetr, and Manam are here, too."

The interview went on for a few minutes more, and then an FJF official interrupted to announce that the opening ceremony was about to begin. As the two teams took their places on the field, Albert focused on his breathing. Already there was a stark difference between the two teams. The Tevs, in complete control of their emotions, stood tall with not a scritch in sight. Albert couldn't get rid of his. And he wasn't alone. Sormie and Wayt were plagued with blue scritches and the hotheaded Doz was topped with a cloud of white.

Two medical drones zipped into place and scanned each player for illegal technological enhancements. Next came the playing of the Tevs' anthem. That eerie, wordless, wailing drone gave Albert the creeps. And then he realized why—it sounded like the music from a horror movie he hated.

When it was time for the Zeenods to sing their anthem, they tried, but with so few Zeenods present, it sounded weak in comparison.

The crests were exchanged and the next thing Albert knew he and Vatria were being asked to step forward.

She was a regal beast. A queen on the field. Her posture was perfect. Her muscular arms, legs, and core were ready for action. As she repeated the FJF vow, her eyes remained locked on the Sñektis in the stands.

Albert felt himself bowing to the FJF officials. But he felt odd—like he was outside his body, watching himself perform. Whatever confidence he had arrived with was fading. He flashed back to the first words Vatria ever said to him. *Albert Kinney of Earth, my vision is superior. Do you know what I can see right now? I can see that you are weak. If you want to survive, quit now.*

Lost in thought, Albert was tapped by the Zhidorian official's tentacle.

"The vow...," the FJF official said.

Forcing himself to look Vatria in the eye, Albert repeated the FJF vow. "As a representative of my planet, I promise to play to the best of my ability, to respect you as my competitor, and to uphold the rules of the game."

Silently, he added the meditation that Kayko had taught him to always include—*May we both play well*. But it was automatic. His focus was splintered.

Vatria leaned forward and whispered, "I have been waiting my entire life for this chance. I will redeem my family's honor." And then she stepped back into line.

Overwhelmed, Albert looked out to see if he could see Lee, his nana, somewhere in the stadium. Send me your ahn, please, he thought.

And then the toss for the kickoff was announced.

The Zeenods won the toss.

Game on.

# 13.1

In his cage in Blocck's office, Tackle was listening to the game—and waiting for Kayko to begin the breakout.

The Z-Tev warden and a number of guards were huddled around the large screen, which was supposed to be showing various views of prison security footage but was now just showing the game. The number of bodies watching made it impossible for Tackle to get even a glimpse of Albert or the Zeenods, but at least he could hear the pregame interviews and would be able to hear the play-by-play. Dying to pace, to shake out his muscles, to run, to jump, to flee, he was on edge in a way that he had never felt before. Every muscle was zinging with desire for action.

Outside the prison, Mehk was also on edge. Wearing his Z-Tev disguise and exterminator uniform, he was standing in the parking lot, pretending to make a call. But he, too, was listening in on the game and waiting for a sign that their huge plan was beginning. Until he saw proof, he couldn't know if the PEERs had been successfully reprogrammed.

On the prison's second floor, Kayko prepared for the big test. Mehk had been smart, she realized, to choose this date and time, because the guards were all in their various offices, glued to the game.

Her bem rippled with both excitement and fear as she walked to her cell door and waved her arms. As usual, the PEER responded instantly. Her cell door opened and the PEER flew in, making the standard announcement: "Behavior change. PEER on alert." The machine then hovered in front of her face, as menacing as always.

She had to give it a voice command to obey her and see if it would work. It was possible that the test would fail, that the PEER would see her as a threat and harm or even kill her, but there was only one way to find out. For so long, she had been locked in here, unable to help her team, her people, her planet. Now she finally had a chance. "PEER, disable your response protocol and obey my commands."

A blue light in the drone's belly blinked three times.

Kayko wasn't sure if it had worked. "PEER, spin around three times." She braced herself for an alarm or the shooting of a net. But the drone spun three times and then hovered, waiting for her next command. Kayko's heart leaped.

"PEER, fly to the ceiling," she said. Up it flew. A laugh burst out. Joyfully, she started to jump around her small cell. "Copy my dance moves, PEER!" she said, and she watched in happy amazement as the drone zipped around, trying to copy her movements.

Quickly, she ran to the small air vent in the wall that the imprisoned Zeenods used to pass their messages, and the drone followed her like a toy pet. She laughed again. "Success! Take control of your PEERs!" she sang out, and then listened as the words were echoed to the next cell.

She ordered her drone to hover by the cell door, and then she watched it zip across the room and stop. This was the drone that she had hated, the drone that had kept its evil eye on her every second of every day since she had been dragged here. She couldn't believe it was now hers.

"PEER, I order you to protect me from all Z-Tevs and Tevs. You will not harm me or hinder my escape," she said. "And now, activate protocol to open cell door and follow me out of this prison."

The cell door whooshed open. Just a minute ago, the drone would have reacted to this act with force. Now, it simply followed her as she stepped out into the hallway.

Relief flooded every muscle. And then she heard it—the whooshing open of cell door after cell door. She turned her head to see Zeenods taking their first steps toward freedom.

"PEER, escort me safely to the main exit," she said. In a beautiful echo, she heard the same command being given by all the other Zeenods.

And then, with pounding hearts, they began to walk.

An alarm went off.

"Keep walking," Kayko said.

In Blocck's office, Tackle's ears perked. The alarm was a good sign.

A computerized voice came through the central communication speaker. "PEER malfunction."

"Go check it out," Blocck said to the guard on his right.

Immediately after the guard walked out, another warning came through. "Security alert. Cell door malfunction. Initiate lockdown."

"What the—" Blocck stood up, angry now. "All of you!" he screamed at the other guards. "Don't just sit there. Go fix whatever's going wrong!"

# 13.2

The trumpet blared. The moment Albert's foot touched the ball, a chaos of lights pulsed from every direction. After a moment, he realized what was going on. All the Tevs and Z-Tevs in the dark stadium—the fans, the vendors, the players on the bench—were glowing at the same time and in the same way, all pulsing with a strobelike pattern of lights. It was like they were all screaming the same distracting song except with light instead of sound. Albert saw the chaos through a gathering blue cloud of scritches. As he was processing the scene, Vatria easily dove in to take the ball.

"Ignore the lights," Ennjy called out to Albert. "Focus on the field."

Almost dizzy, Albert tried to focus on the purple of the ball, the gold of the Zeenods, and the silver of the Tevs. Stay calm, he told himself, still standing at the center midline. As he started to sort out the colors and shapes on the field, he could see that none of the Tevs had scritches around them. Sormie and Wayt, though, were clouded with blue scritches like him. At least he wasn't the only anxious one on the field.

For the first ten minutes or so, the fast and tireless Tevs purposefully made long runs and passes, getting the Zeenods to chase them, hoping to wear them out. But the Zeenod defenders were holding strong.

Suddenly, Feeb won the ball and quickly moved it to Giac, who sent it to Doz. Preparing to make a run, Albert dodged his marker and ran into an open position. He called out, but then he saw Doz send the ball sailing away from his run to the other side of the field, where a cloud of blue light was buzzing—buzzing in front of a Tev.

"Here!" Albert shouted.

Too late.

The Tev player received Doz's gift and played a long, clean pass to the Tev winger, who lifted a ball in to Vatria—who headed it on target. The crowd was roaring.

Chest tight with anxiety, Albert kept his eyes glued to the purple glow that was sailing toward the net, but then Toben dove, stretched his arms. *Phew!* Ball caught!

The Tevs in the stands hissed and sent out messages with flashes of light. Albert was thinking he was happy he couldn't read any of those messages when Doz called out, "I saw the blue scritches and thought it was Albert! Be on guard, team!"

As the game continued, Albert watched carefully, wondering if that Tev player had deliberately become anxious to make the scritches come to him so he would look like Albert. A smart trick, he had to admit.

The game resumed and, sure enough, the same trick happened.

This time it was Giac who was fooled into sending the ball to a Tev player who was shrouded with blue scritches. Clearly Giac thought she was passing to Sormie.

"Shouldn't this be illegal?" Albert yelled.

"We've got to communicate!" Ennjy cried out. "Don't assume blue scritches equals Albert or a Zeenod!"

The next fifteen minutes were a back-and-forth fight for possession. Both teams were playing hard, fighting for their planets and defending for their lives, keeping each other from getting any decent shots.

And then the Tevs broke out. Vatria dropped back into the midfield to receive the ball and used her speed and skill to slalom through defenders on her way toward the top of the box. Beeda was ready.

Go, Beeda, Albert thought. But then a Tev winger brushed by Beeda and—something happened. Albert couldn't see clearly, but Beeda seemed to just stop.

*Bam!* Vatria slammed the ball into the net.

Goal! One to zero, Tev.

It all happened so fast.

The crowd went crazy, but the Tev players stayed focused. No crowd-pleasing victory moves or waves to the crowd. All business.

"We'll get the next one," Ennjy called out, and the game continued.

The Zeenods kept possession, calling out to each other and putting the Tevs on edge.

Albert could see a perfect play coming, and he ran to position himself. Sure enough, the ball went from Heek to Giac to Doz, and now the purple globe was flying toward him. A perfect pass. Albert prepared to receive it. Out of the corner of his eye, he could see the silver glow of a Tev defender coming, but he braced himself for the fight and knew he could own the ball. But then the Tev barely brushed up against him and suddenly Albert's whole left side received the jolt of an electric shock.

Albert cried out and stumbled.

The Tev player who had bumped up against him scooped the ball and kept running.

Albert was confused. Had he just been shocked or was it his imagination?

"Go, go, go!" Ennjy shouted.

Albert ran, chasing the trail of the ball, trying to shake off the strange sensation in his body.

The play resumed, but just as Albert was about to receive another ball, he got another electric jolt from a Tev player. This time it was clear. As Albert recovered, the Tev defender stole the ball and passed it to his center mid, and Doz raced in to pressure. Then, clear as could be, Albert heard Doz cry out, too.

The game continued.

Albert ran near Doz. "They're doing something, right? Giving us shocks?"

"Yes! I thought it was my mind playing tricks!"

After a few minutes of play, Feeb received a shock, too, and relayed his concern to Ennjy.

"They're shocking us!" Albert yelled.

"Definitely!" Giac called.

"Enhancement!" Ennjy called out to the ref, stopping the game.

The Tevs in the crowd went insane.

The Tev tactician, Hissgoff, marched up to Ennjy. "What's your accusation?"

The ref stepped between them, and an FJF official ran in.

Ennjy looked out at her teammates. "How many of you have received shocks?"

Almost every Zeenod raised a hand.

"I don't know how they're doing it, but the Tevs have found a way to give us electric jolts," she said.

Albert suddenly recalled witnessing a scene between Hissgoff and Vatria on Zeeno after a practice. Vatria had made mistakes during practice and Hissgoff had punished her by sending a jolt through her hands. The sight had given Albert the heebie-jeebies. Quickly Albert spoke up, relaying the information.

"We aren't shocking anyone. What do you think we are, grythers?" Hissgoff laughed.

"This is a serious accusation," the FJF official said.

"We'd see evidence of players being hurt if this was happening!" Hissgoff said. "They all look alive to me!"

"The shocks are not enough to harm us," Ennjy said. "Just enough to make us stop for a moment."

"They're just trying to find an excuse," Hissgoff said calmly. "Go ahead and run scans on any of my players. All my players. We have nothing to hide."

The FJF officials initiated the scan, and a drone flew in and orbited each Tev player while the Tevs and their allies in the stands booed and hissed.

Albert caught Vatria talking with Hissgoff, probably agreeing on whatever lie they were going to try to use to cover up the cheat. He felt anger rising and sensed the gathering of white scritches.

"No impairments, viruses, or technological enhancements detected," the scanning drone said.

Albert couldn't believe it.

Cheers rose from the Tevs and their allies in the stands.

And then Feeb marched up to the team of FJF officials with a cloud of white scritches buzzing over his head. "We are not lying! In this history of johka tournaments, this is the most un—"

"Feeb, no!" Ennjy said, too late.

The ref tapped Feeb's right shoulder with the foul-marking sensor. A yellow stripe appeared on his uniform, and the Tevs cheered.

And then the studious, normally calm Feeb turned to Hissgoff and shouted, "Unjust! Unfair! Un—"

Swiftly, the ref's hand came down and a red stripe glowed on Feeb's uniform.

The crowd went wild as Feeb was escorted off the field.

"I can't believe that was Feeb," Giac said.

"I can't believe that wasn't me," Doz said.

Ennjy called out, "We will rise above it!"

# 13.3

Outside the prison, Mehk's spirits had been sinking as he listened to the johka game. He had no doubt the Zeenods were telling the truth and wondered how the Tevs were delivering those secret shocks. And then he heard a welcome sound: the prison-wide siren! This was brilliant! The prison breakout was happening!

He glued his eyes to the main entrance, hoping at any moment to see Tackle and Kayko and the other Zeenods streaming out. The seconds ticked by. And then a side emergency door popped open and a figure ran toward the parking lot. She was the same Z-Tev medic who had killed his gheet!

"What's going on?" Mehk called out, picking up his extermination equipment, pretending he was just about to head inside.

"Save your skin!" the medic said, glancing at him from the eye in the back of her head as she kept running. "There's a breakout. It's going to be a nightmare!"

Mehk smiled. Ha! This was very good news indeed.

# 13.4

As the game continued without Feeb, Albert found himself constantly burning with both anger and anxiety, automatically wincing whenever he came near a Tev. He thought focus would be impossible to regain, but then Reeda successfully blocked a shot and finally got possession. The Zeenods rallied. She passed to Giac.

"Heek!" Giac said, preparing to send the ball to Heek, but as the Tev defenders swarmed toward Heek, Giac sliced it back to Doz, who was trying to cover for Feeb.

Vatria was on it, though, and she swooped in and neatly tapped the ball away just as Doz was about to connect with it. Quickly she dribbled and passed to her right winger. This sent Wayt and Beeda running. As space opened up, the Tev winger passed it square to their midfielder while Vatria ran to the top of the box.

Albert could suddenly see Vatria's pattern of lights too clearly. She was wide open. But then Reeda was rushing toward her just as Vatria was receiving the ball. A Tev winger was close behind Reeda. Go, Reeda! She was going to be in position to handle the play—but then the winger brushed by Reeda and in the next instant Reeda was on the ground.

With one clean strike, Vatria swept the ball in.

Goal! Two to zero, Tev.

The Tev fans cheered.

Giac ran to Reeda's side, bem flying.

"I was definitely shocked," Reeda said to the ref, who brushed her off.

Suddenly a commotion pulled Albert's attention to the Tevs. Vatria had run off the field and was talking to Hissgoff again. A cloud of white scritches were gathering over her head.

"They're arguing about something," Ennjy said.

"After just winning her second goal, I would think she'd be happy," Sormie said.

The game wasn't stopping, though, and they were close to the end of the first half.

The ball floated toward the center for the kickoff, and Vatria hustled to take her place across from Albert, blue scritches now gathering around her eyes and ears—an uncommon sight among their players.

Just before play resumed, Albert was shocked to see Vatria lock eyes with him. As those strange red eyes with those bolt-shaped pupils drilled into his, she whispered, "I overheard a player. They're cheating, but Hissgoff is denying it. At the half, I'm talking to the FJF officials. I want to win, but I want to win fairly."

Albert was stunned, but he had no time to think or share what he had heard. The game restarted. Quickly he passed the ball to Sormie and watched Vatria turn and run.

"Play strong, Zeenods!" Ennjy called out. But she looked exhausted and her voice sounded thin.

Quickly, the Tevs got and kept possession, pulling off the same long runs and passes that they started off the game with. Now up 2–0 while the Zeenods were a player down, they were oozing with cockiness, and their fans loved it.

Albert was struggling. Part of him was just hoping they could get to the half without the Tevs scoring again. And then a shock of a different kind happened. The Tevs had possession and Vatria was about to receive the ball when the two Tev wingers also ran in from either side.

*Smack!* Vatria went down in a bone-crunching hit, crushed between her own teammates.

She didn't move.

The play stopped and Hissgoff ran onto the field, faking concern as the medics swooped in. The two Tev players hovered over Vatria, pretending it was an accident.

"It looked like they took her down!" Ennjy whispered. "Why?"

"She told me the Tevs are cheating," Albert whispered back. "She was going to tell the FJF at the half."

As Vatria's limp body was carried off the field, Albert felt like he was going to vomit. He had been so wrong about her. Yes, she had talked tough and fought hard when they had played against each other before, but really, her behavior on the field was fair. He flashed back to a moment in the Zeenod stadium parking lot after he and the Zeenods had won the first game against the Tevs. Vatria and her Skell elders had stopped by to congratulate them on their way to their ITV. Like her grandfather, Vatria had bowed to him and the Zeenods to express their respect. This was a kind of sportsmanship the Tev players hadn't shown.

He looked around at the blank expressions on the fierce faces of the Tevs. He couldn't imagine playing for a team that would take out one of its own players.

"Look!" Giac said, and gestured to the stadium. The Sñektis who had come to the game to cheer for Vatria were protesting.

"I've never seen anything like this," Ennjy said.

The ball floated into place for the restart of play, but then the halftime trumpet blared.

# 13.5

Inside the prison, Kayko led the Zeenods on her floor down the stairs to the first-floor hallway. When she opened the door, she came face to face with a guard.

"Freeze!" the guard said, fumbling for her weapon, shocked that the prisoners' PEERs were not stopping them.

"PEER, net this guard!" Kayko commanded. Before the guard could react, a smartnet flew out from one of the PEER's robotic arms and wrapped the guard in a tidy cocoon.

In the next moment, streams of Zeenods from the first and third floors were arriving to join them.

"We stopped a guard!" one Zeenod said.

"We did, too!" another said. And another and another.

Kayko's smile was huge. "They assume the PEERs will protect them, not us. We have to hurry while we still have this element of surprise."

"To freedom!" a Zeenod shouted.

"To freedom!" they all chanted.

# 13.6

As Albert followed his teammates into the locker room, he felt pain and exhaustion sink in. Every nerve, muscle, and bone in his body was hurting. He could see it, too, in the plodding footsteps of the Zeenods and even in the way their bems hung heavy from their shoulders.

No one said what Albert believed they were all thinking: there was no hope. One by one they began to pick up smoothies and nurse their wounds. Feeb, now regretting his outburst, kept apologizing over and over.

"We can't trust them!" Doz grabbed a smoothie and held it up. "They probably poisoned these!" *Bam!* His smoothie hit the locker room wall.

"I couldn't believe the scan came out clean," Feeb said. "We know they cheated."

"Vatria knew it!" Albert said. "That's why they took her out!"

He told his team exactly what she had said, and then the other Zeenods all began to talk at once.

"Despicable!"

"They have to be stopped."

"Those Tevs are too good at covering up their crimes," Heek said. "It's their word against ours and—"

"But without proof we can't—" Feeb interrupted.

"What are we supposed to do?" Wayt yelled. "Let them get away with this?"

"It's too much!" Sormie said. "We can't win. It doesn't matter how hard we train, how hard we try, if they're going to—"

"We don't have support. We need—" Toben started to say.

"Fans in the stands!" Beeda and Reeda said in unison.

Giac jumped in. "We're missing the ahn and it's—"

The dialogue continued, one team member interrupting the other. When Albert noticed Ennjy sitting alone, silent, he knew they were lost.

After another minute the door opened and a cloaked figure slipped in. Alarmed, Beeda and Reeda lunged to block the intruder, but stopped when she removed her hood.

"Lee?" Ennjy said.

Warmth flooded Albert. A mix of comfort and pride. His grandmother looked strong and beautiful.

"I was going to stay hidden," she said to Albert, "but this is an emergency."

Doz touched her. "You're alive?"

"Alive," Lee said. Quickly she told the story of her rescue, and Albert was congratulated for his bravery.

"I had thought all hope was lost," Lee said. "Right now, you think all hope is lost for this game. But I'm here to tell you it's the Tevs who are in trouble."

"In trouble? They're winning," Sormie said.

"Two to zero is the worst lead to have," Lee said. "Right now they are thinking they're in a great position to win. But you can flip this. Keep them from getting a third and they will begin to lose their confidence. And then all you need is one to really shake them up. Get one, and they will know that all you need is one more to tie."

Ennjy nodded. "This is all true. And they just sacrificed their best player. Think about it. Clearly they're cheating and they kept that fact from Vatria because they knew she wouldn't approve. And because of that, they realized that the only way for them to continue was to get rid of her. That's something they are going to pay for. We can do this."

"The shocks aren't enough to hurt us," Giac said. "They're just enough to startle us. We can withstand them if our minds are prepared for them. Now we're prepared."

"But the shocks are only one problem," Doz said. "Remember, they can use the scritches to trick us, too."

Ennjy nodded. "We need to stay calm and keep the scritches off the field. That will help."

Albert, Sormie, and Wayt all looked at each other, knowing they were the ones who had the hardest time.

"We need to come out strong and shake their confidence," Heek said.

Albert spoke up. "What about parking the bus?"

Lee smiled. "Good idea."

"In Earth soccer," Albert explained, "there's something we call parking the bus. If you took a school bus and put it in front of the goal, your opponents would never be able to score."

"Put eight or nine players on defense," Lee said. "Allow the Tevs to possess, but don't even let them get close enough to try to score."

Doz jumped up and down. "That will be crazy-making. And then *Bam!* We counterattack!"

Ennjy turned to Lee. "Why don't you put aside your disguise and take your place in the VIP box? Lat and Tescorick think they killed you. Showing up will shake them to their core. That will affect the team!"

"Yes!" Lee tossed her cloak aside. "And Giac, regardless of whether we win or lose, meet me in the FJF communication booth after the game but before the awards ceremony. I have an idea and I'll need your help!"

Giac nodded.

"Circle up," Doz said, and the team pulled in. "More than anything, we need the ahn!"

# 13.7

Still locked in a cage in Blocck's office, Tackle could hear the Zeenods' cheers ring out. Instinctively, he barked out his cheer in return.

Blocck didn't notice. The warden was calling for backup, eyes glued to the security footage. Every view showed Zeenods streaming toward the exit with the PEERs humming along above them. Guards had given up their posts and were running out of the prison.

"I'm going to beam into the tank," Blocck told the director of armed forces on the line. "It's parked out front. I'll hold them off with DREDs until you send troops."

Tackle realized what was going to happen. Once outside the prison and in the safety of a tank, Blocck would fire at the main doors, and that would mean anyone near the main entrance would immediately be killed. The PEERs were no match for missiles.

Blocck ended the call and pulled his Z-da out to initiate a szoŭ.

*Grrrr.* Tackle threw himself at the side of the cage and began to bark.

Assuming the zawg would be good protection, Blocck opened the cage door to take him along. When the cage door opened, Tackle flew out. He jumped up on Blocck, snatched the Z-da in his jaws, and ran out into the main hallway. The exit to the parking lot was to the right, and the double doors that led into the prison were to the left. Through the windows of the double doors on the left, Tackle could see Kayko and the Zeenods!

With no other choice than to make a run for the exit, Blocck ran into the hallway.

Tackle turned to stop him. *Grrrrr.* Charging, he leaped into the air just as Blocck fired a shot. Tackle went down at Blocck's feet.

"Idiot!" With one forceful strike, Blocck kicked him and then ran out.

In the next second, the doors to the prison opened, and Kayko called out, *Tackle!*

# 13.8

After halftime was over, Lee walked out with the team, and when the VIPs and the crowd realized she was there, the confusion in the stadium was fabulous. With majestic elegance, she bowed to the crowd and then walked up to take her place next to the other former Star Strikers, just one box away from the presidents' box. A team of reporters swarmed her, and she smiled and said she'd give an interview after the game. Albert could tell that President Tescorick and President Lat were shocked. Their faces, which were projected on the large screen, looked frozen.

"Let's roll and rock!" Doz shouted out.

When Albert took his place, there wasn't a scritch on the field. The lights and commotion in the stands were even more chaotic, but the familiarity of the chaos along with the ahn-producing pep talk in the locker room gave Albert the ability to take it in and tune it out.

The Tevs had the kickoff. For Albert, seeing the new Tev striker in place where Vatria should be just hammered home the need to win this game.

The trumpet blew and the Tev player passed the ball back to his center midfielder. Because the Zeenods were down 2–0, the Tevs were expecting them to come out with high pressure. Instead, the Zeenods formed a tight defensive shape and allowed the Tevs to possess the ball in front of them.

The Tevs were delighted to see the Zeenods hanging back and now assumed that they had given up the will to win. Wanting to put on a great show for their fans, the Tevs started to attack. This was the Zeenod game plan! As soon as the Tevs entered the Zeenods' defensive shape, the Zeenods pushed them back.

The Tevs kept passing and passing, looking for ways to break in. Here and there a Tev got close and used a shock, but the Zeenods braced their bodies for the hits and stayed strong. The Tevs were watching their strategy lose its power.

While the core of the team was defending, Albert drifted into a sneaky position at half field, ready for the quick counterattack. Stay calm, Albert said to himself, keeping the scritches away.

After a few more minutes of Tev possession, the chance came. The next time the new striker received the ball, Beeda and Reeda swarmed him, took his shocks without breaking focus, and caused him to cough up the ball. Quickly Beeda secured it and got it to Giac's feet.

After enjoying all the extended possession, the Tevs had forgotten about Albert. Now Giac turned and trusted that he was ready to roll and rock. She sent a long ball over the top. The entire Tev team was stuck in the Zeenod half, so Albert ran to receive the through ball with no one to contend him.

Stay calm, Albert said to himself, connecting with the ball. He still had work to do. After he corralled the ball, he was one-on-one with the keeper, but he could feel the powerful Tevs now sprinting to defend. With several more clean touches, he was at the top of the box. And now the Tev keeper had to make a play. He decided to try rushing forward to close down Albert's angle.

Albert saw both a risk and an opportunity. He waited just long enough for the keeper to leave the box. That chancy delay gave a Tev defender enough time to reach Albert. But Albert was ready. The defender shouldered Albert, hoping the shock would throw him off. But Albert took it and curled a beautiful shot around the keeper to tuck that glowing johka ball clean into the net.

Goal! One to two.

Instantly the Zeenods cheered, and their allies in the stands from Jhaateez, Liöt, Fetr, and Manam began to sing the Zeenod anthem. Masses of happy pink scritches appeared at Albert's feet. Albert danced around, loving the way his movement made the tight swarm of scritches explode outward like little fireworks at his feet.

"Look around!" Doz cried out.

Pink scritches were dancing at the feet of every Zeenod. And, for the first time in the game, a number of Tevs were clouded with blue scritches.

"We're getting to them!" Albert said gleefully. "They're freaking out."

"Stay happy!" Ennjy called out.

"Yes! This is freaky-making!" Doz said, dancing with his scritches.

The ball floated into place and as Albert took his place for the restart, he looked around, noticing how much easier it was to clearly see the Zeenods with the pink clouds puffing at their feet.

The Tevs went at the Zeenods again; and again the Zeenods parked the bus, enjoying every second.

Then Doz muscled through a useless shock from a Tev winger to win the ball deep in Zeenod defensive territory. The ahn was in full flow. Doz knew they could break the Tevs down with their bread and butter—tiki-taka. So he zipped it inside to Reeda. Reeda hit a skip pass to Wayt. After the switch, space opened up in the middle. Wayt delivered a pass to Sormie, who was free and able to turn. She played a quick one-two with Giac to skip past a defender and saw a channel down the right sideline. Heek was flying. Sormie hit a deep diagonal ball that was perfect for Heek's direct run. Heek was getting ready to cross the ball! They needed runners in the box! On fire, Albert sprinted toward the front post, drawing two Tev defenders with him. Meanwhile, Ennjy floated in, unmarked, toward the top of the box, where tons of space was just waiting. Without hesitation, Heek delivered a quality ball on the ground.

Albert and every single Zeenod on the field focused on sending Ennjy the ahn. She stayed cool and smacked a gorgeous one-touch strike into the top right corner of the net.

The Zeenods cheered.

Goal! The game was tied 2–2.

All the Zeenods needed was one more. Just one more.

# 13.9

"Keep moving out!" Kayko shouted at her fellow Zeenods. "I'll join you!" Then she crouched by the dog.

Tackle's ears twitched at the sound of her voice and the feel of her hand on his chest.

When people undergo a terrible accident or near-death injury, they often say that life passes before their eyes. True for dogs, too. Now Tackle was experiencing a flickering of memories in his mind's eye. There he was as a puppy wrestling with Trey. There he was snuggling into the big stuffed bear that served as his dog bed. There he was enjoying the chomp of his favorite dog toy.

There he was the moment when Albert realized he could understand his speech. There he was with Albert jumping on the trampoline, battling the haagoolts, and winning the Skill Show. There they were on Gravespace GJ7 discovering the real Trey! And there he was in Silver Spring, Maryland, sitting side by side with Albert in the sweet peace of the backyard.

Tackle lifted his head.

*Tackle!* Kayko stroked his back.

Starlike specks danced in front of Tackle's eyes but gradually cleared. He began to examine himself. One of the bones in his rib cage was cracked. He could feel it. And his front right paw, too, hurt like heck. He licked the blood and could feel the hole with his tongue. The bullet Blocck had fired had gone right through his paw.

*You were shot!* Kayko said, gently removing the smartskin zawg mask that covered Tackle's face and using it to wrap around the wound.

*Yeah. Lucky for me, that dude has horrible aim,* Tackle said, and rose awkwardly as Zeenods and their PEERs streamed by. *Kayko, I heard Blocck say he will use a tank armed with DREDs against us. We need to stop him before he can get to it.*

Although every part of his body ached, Tackle rose to his feet and limped as fast as possible out the main prison doors. But they were too late. Hovering just above the surface of the road facing the prison doors was a large police vehicle armed with DREDs. The Zeenods who had filled the area in front of the prison were frozen, uncertain what to do.

Blocck's voice came booming from one of the vehicles. "You are surrounded. Return to your cells immediately."

*Heads up,* Tackle whispered to Kayko, *guards on both sides.*

To their right and left were two ITV parking lots. Armed guards who had run from the prison were hiding behind the ITVs, weapons pointed at the gathering Zeenods.

From his place in the lot, Mehk ran to join Tackle and Kayko. According to the PEERs' visual surveillance cameras, a Z-Tev was approaching. Immediately, there was a sickening *whirr* as all the PEERs pivoted and aimed to shoot.

Tackle and Kayko both called out at the same time. *Don't shoot! It's a Zeenod in disguise. It's Mehk!*

Quickly Mehk realized what was happening and ripped off his Z-Tev mask.

The PEERs shifted their focus back to the DREDs, and Mehk took a breath. Regaining his composure, he stood with Kayko and Tackle and turned to face the tank. "Blocck," he called out, holding up his communication device. "I am the Zeenod Mehklen Pahck. This is a Zeenod uprising. I know that you are receiving a message that I am receiving. Prisoners are escaping in ten other prisons. Z-Tev guards are fleeing. This is a planet-wide revolution! You called for backup, but the army can't be everywhere at once."

One of the Z-Tev guards on the ground turned and ran. Another followed.

Blocck's voice bellowed, "Guards, stay at your posts!"

The Zeenods cheered and were about to proclaim victory, but then an ominous shadow appeared overhead. As they watched, dozens of large vehicles appeared in the sky. Army vehicles. Transport units. Each one could carry one hundred soldiers and there were at least thirty vehicles arriving. An army of three thousand.

No one said a word.

What now? Tackle thought.

# 13.10

With twenty minutes left in the tournament, the Zeenods had to get one back while the Tevs were furious and desperate to get back on top.

The ball floated into place and the trumpet blared. For the next ten minutes, it was gridlock. Both teams attacked and defended fiercely. Shots on goal were fired, but both goalies were locked in and impenetrable.

"We're tired, but we can do this!" Ennjy called out.

All the tension, the drama, the pain, the extra pull of the higher gravity made Albert want to sink to his knees, but he knew he needed to dig deeper. This was bigger than a game. This was bigger than a tournament. This was for the future of Zeeno.

In the next ten minutes, both teams started to lose it. Players were cramping up, stumbling, and making inaccurate passes and reckless shots.

In the last minute, though, the Tevs mustered a final attack. They broke through the Zeenod defense and suddenly were in position for the game-winning shot.

From his position at half field, Albert's heart pounded and his throat went dry.

The Tev striker focused on his technique and put his laces through the ball. *Smack!* Beautiful contact. The ball was headed to the bottom left corner of the goal.

Albert was sure it was in.

Then in the blink of an eye, Toben pounced, bem flying, arms outstretched, palms spread wide. *Boom!* A soaring Toben parried the ball away from the net.

What a save!

Reeda swooped in and cleared the ball out of danger.

The Zeenods cheered. The Tevs booed.

The final trumpet blared.

Score tied! Two to two.

"What now?" Albert cried out. "Overtime?"

"There's no overtime in johka," Ennjy said. "We go straight into a shootout. Each team chooses three PK shooters. Whoever scores more wins."

As the ref and the two teams prepared for the final shootout, the noise level in the stadium rose to a mighty roar. The Tevs and their allies began stomping and flashing messages of victory while Zeenod allies stood and belted out the Zeenod anthem.

"Sormie, Doz, and Albert, do you want to take the shots?" Ennjy asked.

Quickly, blue scritches gathered around Sormie. "Thank you for your confidence, Ennjy," Sormie said with a quavering voice. "I'm sorry, but my mind is not right. Take it, please."

Ennjy touched her arm. "No need to apologize."

"I'm ready," Doz said. "Ennjy, you take the first shot."

Ennjy nodded and looked at Albert.

Albert felt panic rise, but he heard himself say he was in.

As the two keepers took their places at the goal, the players on both sides lined up shoulder to shoulder along the midline.

The ref tossed the coin to determine who would kick first.

"Tev," he announced, and the Tevs cheered.

The ball floated into place.

The first Tev to step up was their most skilled midfielder. Throughout the tournament, she had performed with consistently high quality. She looked confident and wasted no time. After taking three large steps back, she struck a shot. It whizzed past Toben's outstretched right hand.

Goal!

Deafening roars coursed through the stadium.

Don't panic, Albert told himself.

The Zeenods were up next. It was time for Ennjy to step up. The ball floated back into place.

But as she walked to the ball, Albert noticed that her step was tired, her bem was stiff, and a few blue scritches were following her. The tension had gotten to her. Ennjy was actually shaken! Albert closed his eyes. He couldn't watch.

In the next moment, Albert heard that massive Tev cheer again. His eyes flew open to see the ball miss, just sailing over the top of the net. It had been a good strong strike, but it had flown just a tad too high. Such things happened, Albert knew. You did your best and sometimes it was off by just an inch.

Ennjy turned, her face draining of its color as she walked back to her teammates. Albert knew that feeling.

"I choked," she said sadly.

Doz squeezed her shoulder. "It happens. We still can do this!" He turned to the team. "The ahn! The ahn!"

Albert realized he had been so anxious when Ennjy was up, he had forgotten to send her the ahn. The Tevs were now up one. He needed to focus—they all needed to stay calm and positive. The cool thing was how simple and stripped-down this fight had become. No tricks or cheating could be pulled here. No advantages or disadvantages of geography or biology. It was just three players, one shot each.

The next Tev was their fiercest winger. She had lightning-quick feet and was near Vatria's equal. Looking smug, she walked up to the spot like the Tevs already had it in the bag. Then she took aim and blasted the ball toward the bottom right corner.

You can do it, Toben! Albert sent every ounce of his energy to the keeper.

Exploding through his toes, bem fully flexed, Toben leaped to his right and stuck out a strong palm to parry the shot wide.

A save!

A burst of positive energy hit Albert and his teammates. Doz was next. If he made this shot it would be back to a tie. The crowd in the stadium hushed. Everyone was on edge.

As Doz stepped up, Albert could feel the ahn flowing. Clearly Doz could feel it, too. He looked back at his teammates with a huge grin as pink scritches flooded his feet. Albert was amazed that he could be in such a euphoric state with so much pressure. And their fans in the stands loved it.

The keeper looked anxious. She started moving frenetically to try to distract Doz from his moment.

Doz. Doz. Doz. Albert focused on his friend.

In a flash, Doz ran to strike hard as if he were going to put a hole in the back of the net. Then, at the last moment, he delicately pulled back some strength in exchange for a cheeky surprise: what Albert would call a perfect Panenka. The keeper dove to his right as the ball floated right down the middle.

Albert and the Zeenods cheered.

Now it was 3–3. The game could be anyone's. Albert could hear and feel and almost taste both the excitement and the panic in the air.

The Tev striker who subbed for Vatria was their final choice. As he walked to the ball, Vatria's fans in the audience began to hiss. The Tev fans increased their rhythmic stomping and the flashing of their victory message.

Albert watched Toben and the striker lock eyes. They both knew this was a massive moment. Inside, Albert could feel himself wishing that something bad would happen to the striker. A slip and fall! A sudden heart attack! A punishing lightning bolt from the sky! And then he stopped himself, knowing that negative energy wasn't going to help. Quickly he turned his attention toward Toben, sending his positive thoughts for strength and focus.

The striker stood tall and began a powerful approach. *Bam!* He hit the ball so hard it echoed through the stadium. Toben dove but had absolutely no chance. The ball was moving too fast. And then…the arc curved just enough and…*BANG!* The ball bounced off the post—the goalie's best friend!—and flew toward the left corner of the field.

The Tev fans booed and the Zeenod fans cheered. Still 3–3.

This was it. The final shot. Albert's turn.

"You've got the ahn," Ennjy said.

"Full steam in the head!" Doz said.

A few blue scritches appeared in front of Albert's face. He looked up at the stands. Even though Lee was too far to see clearly, he knew she was sending her ahnic energy. He could feel it. He knew, too, that all over the Fŭigor Solar System, Zeenods were watching. They, too, were sending him their ahn. Tackle and Kayko and Mehk—they were with him even if they couldn't be here.

Feeling all that ahn flowing from his fingertips to his feet, Albert started his approach. At first he ran, but a few feet before he was ready to strike, he slowed down to mess up the keeper's timing. That slight hesitation sent the goalie diving to his right and leaving the left side of the net wide open. In that nanosecond, Albert could see that all he had to do was stay calm and pass it in. For Zeeno, he thought, and with one firm strike he slotted the ball into the back of the net.

*Zing!*

A surreal silence followed, as if no one in the stadium could believe what had happened.

And then the announcement boomed: "Zeeno wins the game and the tournament."

# 13.11

"Surrender!" Blocck called out. "The Z-Tev army is arriving!"

A chill went through Tackle as the transport vehicles descended to hover over them, but then Mehk smiled. "Look! Those aren't Z-Tev vehicles."

The distinctive crest of the planet Jhaateez became visible on the now-hovering ITVs.

Kayko gasped. "Jhaateez?"

In the next few seconds, a mass szoŭ occurred and thousands of Jhaateezians and Zeenods from Jhaateez materialized among the Zeenods on the ground. The atmosphere suddenly shifted from fear to joy.

"Calm down!" Mehk called out. "This isn't over! Zeenods, activate your PEERs' recording devices!"

As the message quickly passed throughout the crowd, everyone hushed and the cameras on one thousand drones zoomed out and began recording. At the same time, two large missiles were lowered by Blocck into firing position and swiveled to aim at the crowd.

"Blocck!" Mehk stepped out. "Right now, your own PEERs are recording you. We are sending this footage to every planet in the Fŭigor Solar System. There are citizens of Jhaateez now standing here with us. With the solar system watching, are you going to kill us all?"

# 13.12

As Albert and the Zeenods recovered from the shock of winning, the booing and hissing from the Tevs and their allies in the stands became intense.

The Tev team and their tactician Hissgoff stood motionless, clearly not having planned what to do in case of a defeat, while giant screens all over the stadium showed the instant replay of Albert's winning shot.

Lee moved from the VIP box to the FJF communication booth, and Giac rushed over to join her. At the same time, the awards podium was brought out and FJF officials began the awards ceremony.

But as the Fŭigor Johka Federation's director began the opening speech, Giac and Lee worked their tech magic and the giant screens all over the stadium switched from showing a close-up of the podium to broadcasting the prison breakout scene happening on Zeeno.

Suddenly everyone, including the director, hushed and watched as Kayko, Tackle, Mehk, and thousands of Zeenods and allies stood facing Blocck's missiles.

Albert's heart pounded. There they were—all of them—standing together outside the prison!

And then Giac programmed the screen's view to split into twelve other panels. One of those panels showed the footage Lee had recorded on GJ1 of the banished Tevs. The other eleven were showing Zeenods standing outside ten other prisons. Fleets of allies from Manam, Liöt, and Fetr, and the Zeenods who had been living on those planets, were appearing at those locations to stand united with the Zeenods who had escaped.

"Albert, take the microphone," Ennjy said. "Explain what's happening!"

"Me?" Albert asked.

She smiled. "You've seen it all. And without you, we wouldn't have had Tackle or Mehk as our allies."

Albert flashed back to a scene he had imagined, a scene he had thought would be a fantasy: a chance to speak up for Zeeno. Before he could give himself time to get nervous, he walked up to the podium and began to speak.

"I, Albert Kinney of planet Earth, have witnessed the illegal oppression of Zeenods by Tevs and Z-Tevs. Over seventy-five years ago, the Tevs invaded Zeeno, set up a false government, killed or imprisoned innocent Zeenod citizens who rebelled, and—"

A huge roar of anger and protest rose up from the Tevs and Z-Tevs in the stands. "Lies! Lies! Lies!" they began to chant, flashing the message to drown him out. Tev guards from all over the stadium were making their way toward the stage. The noise from the stadium grew more intense.

Out of the corner of Albert's eye, he saw Lee rushing to join him. Albert kept going. "The entire solar system is listening. And here is the truth. We have proof that President Lat has been working for President Tescorick to further oppress the Zeenod people and to allow Tevs and Z-Tevs to ruin the planet's ecosystem. We have proof that Z-Tevs have wrongfully imprisoned Kayko Tusq and thousands of other Zeenods, proof that Tevs have been imprisoning innocent Tevs on GJi, proof that they tried to kill me, to kill my dog, and to kill my grandmother, the former Star Striker known as Lee. The Tevs in power are not leaders. They are murderers."

"Lies! Lies! Lies!" many of the Tevs and their allies from Gaböq and Yurb began to chant, but Albert could tell it wasn't all of the Tev allies shouting. Some had fallen silent.

"This is not the Zeenods' word against the Tevs' word, as the Tevs would want you to believe!" Albert shouted over the chants. "We have witnesses and can present evidence."

Zeenods and their allies cheered.

Albert looked at the image of the prison breakout on the screen. "Kayko! Can you hear me? It's your turn to speak."

Kayko's voice came booming through the system. "We demand the rightful freedom of Zeenods to live and work. We have the right to care for and govern our planet. The time has come. Right now, we are getting word that Z-Tevs are fleeing our planet."

A cheer rose up.

"President Tescorick and President Lat need to be held accountable for the crimes they have committed," she went on.

Tescorick stood, burning with anger. "The Tevs on GJi are criminals, not innocents. And if there are crimes being committed against Zeenods, there is one person to blame—President Telda Lat!"

Albert locked eyes with President Lat, who was sitting next to Tescorick in the VIP box. Her face had gone gray.

A roar went up. The tension in the stadium seemed ready to give way to violence.

Rushing to the podium, the president of the Fŭigor Interplanetary Council held up their tentacled arms. "There will be no violence! Due to the vast numbers of Zeenods and their allies who are involved, we propose that a full and fair investigation needs to be done by the FIC—"

Attention suddenly shifted. The Sñektis in the stadium were rising up and focusing their gazes behind Albert. Turning, Albert saw Vatria limping out onto the field. Holding her side and wincing with every step, she joined Albert as the Sñektis cheered for her. Everyone in the stadium knew that the fact that she was still injured meant that either her injuries were so bad they couldn't be repaired or the Tevs had denied her medical care. Either way, the Tevs were to blame.

She and Albert locked eyes. She nodded, and then she spoke into the microphone. "I, too, have witnessed crimes committed by the Tevs. They were using illegal means to try to win this game. When they learned that I couldn't agree, they deliberately injured me. I stand with the Zeenods."

The crowd was stunned into silence.

Vatria lifted her chin. "The Sñekti culture has much in common with the Tev culture. We are hardworking, ambitious, and highly skilled. But as a Sñekti, I have taken a vow to play fair and am proud of that vow. The Tev leadership no longer deserves our support. I encourage the President of Sñekti and all Sñektis to change allegiance. Zeeno deserves our support."

All eyes turned to the VIP box. The president of Sñekti stood and bowed in agreement. A murmur went through the stadium.

Having Sñekti join with Manam, Liöt, Fetr, and Jhaateez in allying with Zeeno meant they would have a majority. Albert looked over at Vatria, beaming with gratitude.

She nodded and stepped back.

The president of the Fǔigor Interplanetary Council turned to the presidents in the VIP box. "How many agree with the proposal of a full and fair investigation?"

The old allies of Zeeno immediately raised their hands, and the president of Sñekti joined them.

The FIC president held up a tentacle. "Majority in favor. Immediate authorization to send neutral investigative troops to both Zeeno and GJ1."

A cheer went up.

Albert knew that as soon as those troops arrived—with the entire solar system now watching—the truth would be revealed.

"We request the full cooperation of President Tescorick and President Lat," the FIC president added.

President Tescorick turned to consult his advisors, but President Lat stood and began to walk to the podium.

A little chill went through Albert as he watched her approach the microphone. Her bem had stiffened and her gaze was set, as if she were looking at something in the distance. This was the same

Zeenod who had put Kayko into prison, the same Zeenod who had been so willing to send him flying into a black hole, so willing to get rid of anyone in her path. They locked eyes for a split second as she turned to face the crowd. Her expression was hard to read. Then she leaned in and spoke.

"Albert Kinney is correct. I have been working for the Tev leadership," she said, and the crowd hushed again. "President Tescorick made it very clear that unless I did whatever was asked of me, I would be killed."

"Liar!" Tescorick screamed.

"Whatever I did, I did because my own life was threatened," she went on. "As president of Zeeno, I request that the Fŭigor Interplanetary Council oversee temporary leadership of Zeeno. I hereby resign and am turning myself in."

Lat looked over at Albert and the Zeenod team. There was no warmth or compassion or shame or regret in her eyes. She was simply calculating her odds for personal survival. That was what she had always done, Albert realized. To survive, she had worked for the Tevs. Now that the power was shifting, the only way for her to survive was to cooperate.

Tescorick protested, but the FIC president ordered guards to detain him and to strip the Tev guards of their weapons. "The Fŭigor Interplanetary Council will hereby oversee temporary leadership for both Tev and Zeeno until the investigation is complete."

The cheers from the Zeenods and their allies were deafening.

As Tescorick and Lat were escorted out of the stadium, the Fŭigor Johka Federation officials stepped forward with the gold medals.

Albert couldn't help himself. "By the way," he said to the FIC president. "President Lat stole my gold medal from the first game. I'd like that back."

# 13.13

*To Earth?* Tackle asked as they all headed to the stadium lot.

*Not yet,* Doz said. *Party time!*

They all boarded a jumbo ITV provided by the Fŭigor Johka Tournament to return to Zeeno for a formal post-tournament celebration.

Right after takeoff, Doz turned on some music and they all unbuckled and began to dance, Zeeno style, which resembled duckwalking to Albert. Lee joined in, which was even more hilarious. Albert was still astonished that his nana was Lightning Lee.

"I am too joyfilled to hibernate!" Doz said.

"Us too," Beeda and Reeda said.

But the extraordinary energy that they had put out to win the game finally caught up with them, and after a while the hyggs popped out and the entire ITV went silent except for the purrs and clicks of the vehicle's systems. Time passed in that surreal way that it always did during hibernation, and then Sormie shouted a wake-up call.

"Z-Tev vehicles!" she cried out in alarm.

Albert raced out of his hygg. Through the observation window, the approach to Zeeno was visible, and streaming away from Zeeno were hundreds of Z-Tev vehicles.

"Wait. Let's not panic," Ennjy said as several zoomed past. "They aren't coming to get us. They're leaving Zeeno."

Feeb's eyes lit up. "The Z-Tevs must know that the power has shifted! They are probably afraid of the coming investigation."

There were shared, excited glances as they all realized what was happening. The Tev occupation was falling apart. The dream they had been working toward for the past seventy-five years was finally coming true! Although Albert had thought they might cheer, the atmosphere inside the ITV hushed as they belted in for the approach.

"Landing successful," the computer said as they touched down in the center of the stadium's field. "Prepare for exit."

Without speaking, they gathered at the hatch. Surrounded by his teammates, Albert could feel the bems rippling, the ahn flowing, and an almost unbearable anticipation.

"Hatch opening," the computer said. "Please wait for the staircase to lock into place before descending."

With a whoosh, the hatch lifted, and a blast of Zeeno air blew in and sent the sound of bems rustling throughout the cabin. The stadium glowed before them, packed with Zeenods. On the stage directly across from their vehicle stood the three official greeters: Tackle, Kayko, and Mehk.

Albert's heart leaped, and then, before the formal procession could begin, Tackle took off running toward him. Since his paw had been healed through fehkhatting, he raced like a champion. Even though Albert was supposed to wait for the trumpet and then walk down with his team, he couldn't stand still.

"Tackle!" Albert raced down the steps and crouched to throw his arms around his friend. There was Tackle's warm face against his neck and the feel of his living, breathing body in his embrace. "It's so good to see you again!" He took Tackle's face in his hands and looked into his caramel-colored eyes. There was such love reflecting back, love that felt as vast as the space Albert had just flown through. *You took so many risks for me, Tackle,* Albert choked, *risks that I shouldn't have let you—*

Tackle's tail thumped twice. *Albert, I chose to take those risks. I wanted to take those risks.*

Albert smiled and hugged him again, and then the entire team

221

was racing down the stairs. "Tackle!" Doz cried, diving in for a hug.

The trumpet blared.

"Let's go, team!" Lee cried out.

Albert stood and wiped his eyes while Tackle planted his paws down and shook out his muscles. And then they both joined his team to walk toward the stage.

Kayko was beaming, eyes gold, bem lengthening. Standing tall, Mehk was smiling too, nervous but happy.

One by one, they walked up the long ramp to the stage, the crowd cheering without stop.

When they were all in place, Kayko raised both fists in the air. "We are here to celebrate not only the winning of the johka tournament, but also the reclamation of Zeeno."

Another cheer went up. Six gold ITVs circled over the field; their doors opened and vacha blossoms began to float down. The traditional Zeenod confetti!

The crowd went wild. Faces tilted to the sky to catch the delicious feathery, pinkish-white petals that were falling like snowflakes. Tackle ran in circles, tongue slurping up to catch the treats.

And then another set of ITVs flew in and everyone stopped and looked up.

As the vehicle doors opened, multicolored ahda birds took to the sky.

The crowd hushed as the birds began their murmuration. The shape of the infinity symbol appeared in the sky. Albert looked at Lee, who was drinking in the beautiful sight.

As the ahdas continued their symbolic dance, they began to sing that ancient and ethereal birdsong. Gently, the bems of all the Zeenods around Albert and Tackle and Lee began to respond, extending and moving, and everyone sang the wordless chant with the birds. Albert could feel the power of the moment. In the stands were Zeenods who had been relegated to the zones and Zeenods who had been released from prisons and Zeenods who had returned from other planets. They were together for the first time in decades. All eyes glowing gold.

Suddenly, as if the movements of the ahdas were a giant hand lifting them, Albert felt the ground give way. Along with everyone around him, he rose a few inches off the ground. A wild, joyous laugh rippled out. And then, with a great joyful crescendo, the birds scattered into the winds, and Albert and the Zeenods gently thumped back onto the ground.

"And now our expression of gratitude," Kayko said, and the audience sat down. "On behalf of planet Zeeno, we would like to award the Zeeno medal of honor to those who have helped on this journey toward freedom. Our first medal goes to Star Striker Vatria Skell."

From the VIP seating section, Vatria stood and walked over to receive her medal.

"I am deeply honored," she said with a bow.

Over her shoulder, Albert could see her grandfather Paod Skell looking on with pride.

"Next, our former Star Striker Lightning Lee, who has been working for Zeeno for decades."

Lee stepped forward.

"Some of you may not know this," Kayko went on. "But Lee has been secretly protecting Zeenod plant and bird species from extinction by caring for them in a safe environment on Earth. Technically, this is a violation of one of the FJF's most important rules." A murmer went through the crowd, and Kayko held up her hand. "Today, I am happy to report that the Fŭigor Interplanetary Council has decided to pardon Lee. They said her work was an emergency service for the greater good of Zeeno." Eyes turning gold, she put a medal around Lee's neck. "We are grateful for all you've done for us."

"I have known this day would come." Lee's smile was huge. "This is the beginning of a jubilant return for all Zeenods and for the health and well-being of the entire planet. I will begin transporting the seeds and birds back to Zeeno, where I know they will prosper."

Kayko spoke again. "The medal also goes to our ahnuru Ennjy and to every Zeenod on the johka team."

Albert beamed as he watched each player step up to receive the new medals from their beloved coach. The teammates had become friends: wise Ennjy, funny Doz, clever Giac, sweet Sormie, serious Feeb, quiet Heek and Wayt, strong Beeda and Reeda, and trustworthy Toben.

Ennjy smiled. "On behalf of the team, we would like to say that we have been honored to serve."

"Next," Kayko said, "we honor those who came to our aid at crucial times. The Tevs who were on Gravespace GJ1 helped Albert and Lee escape. Accepting the award on behalf of these courageous Tevs is Devrik Tok."

Lee's old opponent stepped forward, so overwhelmed with emotion, she could only bow.

"Another individual on a different gravespace also came to our aid on two different occasions." Kayko looked around. "Was Laika able to come?"

Tackle's ears perked. He knew he smelled zawg. And then Laika was trotting up the steps to the stage.

Tackle waited until she got the medal and then ran over to greet her.

Kayko went on. "We also would like to extend a special medal to Zeenod Mehklen Pahck for the courage to return his allegiance to Zeeno." Kayko smiled warmly at Mehk. "He also violated rules, but the FIC has agreed on a pardon. His ability and willingness to reprogram the drones called PEERs was crucial to the success of the revolution."

Mehk bowed his head to receive the medal, and then suddenly his gaze snapped up. "I have an idea! I can reprogram the PEERs to carry and plant seeds all over Zeeno." Wildly excited, Mehk looked at Lee and Kayko and then Albert. "Ha! A fleet of seed-shooters! It's brilliant, isn't it?"

It was a brilliant idea, Albert thought. And now that he was working for Zeeno, Mehk would undoubtedly have many more brilliant ideas to help restore Zeeno to health.

Kayko put her hand on Mehk's shoulder and said, "Glad to have you on our team!" She turned to Albert. "And finally, medals of honor go to our current Star Striker Albert Kinney and his partner, Tackle."

Albert stepped up with Tackle now at his side. Kayko was thin—the result of imprisonment—but her gaze was as strong and powerful as when Albert first met her. She hugged him and put the medal around his neck. And then she did the same with Tackle.

Albert's johkadin was projected and the stadium cheered.

Ennjy came forward. "We have new Z-das for Albert and Lee. Star Strikers are always welcome to return to the Fŭigor Solar System. In addition, Albert, we hope we can count on you to play in next year's tournament."

Albert took the new Z-da in his hand. He had been so focused on getting through this year's tournament and revolution, he hadn't even thought about the future. The idea that he could return and play with the teammates he loved made him want to shout with joy. "Yes!" he said. "Yes!"

Lee gave his shoulder a squeeze.

"And now, we celebrate!" Kayko said.

# 13.14

After the party, a new ITV was waiting to carry Albert, Tackle, and Lee back to Earth. And when Albert saw the chaperone standing in the hatch, he grinned. "Unit B?" He turned to Lee. "This looks like my first chaperone. She used to call me out for all my shawbles. She threw herself on that explosive johka ball to save my life!"

"Welcome, Albert Kinney," the robot bowed. "I am indeed Unit B33QX920J63434."

As they entered the vehicle, she walked to the control panel, slapped her hip, and ratcheted into a sitting position of perfect posture—without the need of a chair.

"You're back!" Albert said, suppressing a desire to hug the thing.

The robot's head swiveled to look at Albert with a familiar black-eyed stare. "Yes, Albert. My central processing unit was recovered and has been uploaded to an armature that resembles the Unit B you knew. Do you like the way I look or would you prefer to see a body-form menu?"

Albert laughed. "It's good to see you, Unit B! Don't change a thing."

"In that case, prepare for takeoff." The robot abruptly spun around and began tapping the control panel with slender metal fingers.

Buckled in, the three Earthlings sat facing the rear observation window, watching Zeeno grow smaller and smaller.

"You know, Albert, school will be out soon," Lee said. "Maybe you should spend the summer with me in New Zealand. You could help me transport the seeds and birds back to Zeeno."

*Grrr,* Tackle said, *New Zealand sounds too far away.*

Albert laughed and reached over to rub Tackle's ears.

"You know, your Z-da works on Earth, Albert," Lee said.

Albert looked over. "What do you mean?"

She smiled. "You can activate the szoŭ at lunchtime in New Zealand and time-fold to be back in Maryland in time for a second lunch."

"You're kidding?"

"Nope. How do you think I kept my place running in New Zealand the whole time I was in Maryland?"

A glimpse of Albert's new life stretched out in his mind's eye. He could travel whenever and wherever he wanted. "Will all my implants keep working?"

She nodded. "You'll definitely get straight As in Spanish and any other language you take. And you'll be able to withstand crazy temperatures and breathe underwater and all that good stuff."

Albert grinned.

"You still have to follow the rules, though," she went on. "You can't tell a soul, Albert. And you can't bring anything from the Fŭigor Solar System back to Earth. You heard what the FIC said in their pardon—they ruled that my saving the seeds and birds was an emergency service for the greater good of Zeeno."

"I'll follow the rules," Albert said. "I don't want anything to get in the way of me continuing on as Star Striker."

She gave his arm a squeeze.

*Ding!* The bell rang signaling it was safe for them to unbuckle. Albert unbuckled and released Tackle as Nana stood and stretched.

"I think it's hygg time," she said. "I'm looking forward to a nice four-day hibernation!" She popped open her hygg and it floated into place. "Want me to get yours ready?"

"I'll do it in a minute," he said, bending over to give Tackle a rubdown.

She planted a kiss on the top of his head. "See you guys later."

"Wait." Albert looked at the dark expanse through the window. "Do you think the Tev leadership will try to get support from their allies like Gabŏq and Yurb and fight to keep control? Like an all-out war?"

"I hope not," she said. "But one thing is certain. The Zeenods and all those Tevs like Devrik who have been oppressed are finally being heard. I believe they'll have way more support than the Tevs who believe in Tescorick."

Albert nodded.

"Promise you'll get some rest soon?" she asked.

"Promise," he said.

She gave them each a hug and then ducked into her hygg.

Albert sat on the floor closer to the window, and Tackle trotted over to sit next to him.

After a few minutes, Unit B shifted into autopilot, and then it was just the hum of the vehicle and Tackle's calm panting. Albert looked in the distance, wondering how many other planets were out there, each rotating around their own sun, each vibrating with life that was experiencing its own sets of joys and sorrows.

*Just think, Tackle. We're a tiny part of one solar system, which is part of one galaxy, but there are billions of galaxies. Maybe trillions. Nobody even knows how many.*

Tackle put a paw on Albert's arm. *Thanks for making me feel small.*

Albert laughed. *Lots of people on Earth think we're alone.*

Tackle's tail thumped against the floor. *If they knew what we know, it would blow their minds.*

*Totally,* Albert agreed.

"Clarification," Unit B turned to face them. "Knowing a fact cannot make one's mind explode."

Albert smiled. "We'll remember that."

Tackle snorted, and they both turned their attention back to the window. Staring into the mysterious darkness of space was addictive.

*Seriously, Tackle. Could you imagine being the type of leader who would see another planet and decide to take it over and ruin the lives of the people who call that planet home?*

Tackle shook his head. *And don't forget about the lives of the dogs who call it home.*

Albert smiled. *Right. We can't forget about the lives of dogs and zawgs and gheets and gnausers, either.*

Tackle nodded his approval.

*If I discovered a new planet, I'd think I'd try to learn from it,* Albert said.

Something like a laugh came out of Tackle.

*What?* Albert looked at him.

*Well, that's exactly what you did, dude. You went to Zeeno and learned not just how to play johka, but how to be stronger, braver, wiser.*

Albert grinned. *Thanks, Tackle!* He put his arm around the dog. *But what if I could learn more? Like about Z-da technology and time-folding? What if I could use what I learn and apply it on Earth? What if there are things I could learn from Zeeno that could help Earth?*

*As Mehk would say, brilliant!* Tackle put up a paw for a fist bump, and then they both looked out the window again.

Albert tried to picture what was happening on Zeeno right now. There was probably a planet-wide party going on. Zeenods would be reuniting, reclaiming, and rebuilding. During games, Albert had felt the extraordinary exhilaration that came when ahnic energy was flowing between the Zeenod fans and players in a huge stadium; yet, that was nothing compared to the ahn that must be flowing on the planet now. The ahn must be off the charts. He closed his eyes. Just thinking about it activated the ahn in him. He took a breath in and let it out, focusing his attention on the warm buzz of all that positive energy.

*What are you doing?* Tackle asked.

*Feeling the ahn,* Albert said, eyes still closed. The memory of his first huddle with the Zeenods came to him. With invisible threads of positive energy, their souls had connected. A sudden rush of love and gratitude brought tears to his eyes.

Tackle, sensing he needed a moment, simply nuzzled closer.

Albert took another breath and let it out.

After all these adventures, after all these lessons learned, he was going home. He could hardly believe it. A break from the high-stakes tension would be good. He could have some ordinary fun hanging out with friends. And Jessica. He thought back to the heart-felt message he had left for her and wondered if she had liked it. Maybe there would be a reply waiting for him when he got home. And there was his family. Now that he knew his mom wasn't dating Mr. Sam, he could relax. He could teach Erin some soccer moves and keep up training with Tackle in the park. And then he could take some crazy, secret trips to help his nana.

Life was going to be good. And knowing that life for the Zeenods was also going to be good made him tingle with pride. Albert opened his eyes and looked at Tackle. *I'll be happy to be home again.*

Tackle nodded. *I'll be happy to smell home again.*

Albert laughed. *That, too.*